Also by Jax Hunter

TRUE HEROES SERIES

True Valor
True Courage
True Honor
True Virtue
True Gallantry

For special announcements, coupons and insider information, join Jax's email list at books.byjax.com

Please stop by her website and Facebook:
JaxMHunter.com
AuthorJaxHunter.com

JAX HUNTER

True Heroes: True Valor
by Jax Hunter

© 2016 by Jax Hunter

All rights reserved. No part of this book may be used or reproduced, graphic, electronic, or mechanical, including photocopying, recording, taping, or by any information storage retrieval system without the written permission of the author.

Published by **Battle Road Books**

This book is a work of fiction. People, places, events, and situations are creations of the author's imagination. Any resemblance to actual persons, living or dead, or historical events, is purely coincidental.

To friends that stick by you, even when they're not sure you're innocent.

Prologue

If Mac remembered correctly, there was an old *MASH* episode where one of the commanders was leaving, and since all the medical personnel were in surgery, there was no one to say goodbye.

And here he was at his own hail and farewell, sitting by himself, nursing a pitcher of whatever was on tap. It would take him all night at this rate.

Lily had dropped him off, wanting to spend her last evening in California with Daniel. She still worried about her dear friend from SAR. Since Karen's death, he'd gone into a shell—not that, to Rick's mind, the boy had ever been all that out of a shell—and Lily wondered frequently if he'd ever be the same.

Rick didn't want to interrupt her time with him.

Tomorrow, they'd be off to Colorado. By way of the Caribbean, where they'd get hitched. Tonight wasn't just a going away party that didn't happen. It was the only bachelor party he'd have.

The nerve of the Coast Guard to call for help from his teams. Tonight, of all nights.

Technically, they weren't his teams any more. Now, they belonged to Tom Scott. Tom's first command. He seemed to be a good guy.

As if conjured from his thoughts, the new commander appeared. Rick poured him a beer.

"Sorry about your party, Mac. I stopped by to see if you'd gotten the word."

"It's highly irregular for us to be meeting like this, Tom."

Tom actually blushed, which helped lighten Rick's mood.

"I was joking."

"Oh."

"Sit. Drink. If I finish this by myself, Lily will kill me."

Tom glanced around the room. "Where is she tonight?"

"With a friend."

"Ah, Fraser?"

"God, you're up to speed awfully quick."

Tom shrugged off the statement, clearly not sure if Mac had meant it as a compliment or another joke. Rick himself wasn't sure. It was hard to turn your family over to a new dad.

"You know, they're an extremely tight group," Rick said.

"Who?"

"The teams."

"Oh, right. Yeah, seems like it."

Rick downed another swallow of beer along with the emotion that had accumulated in his throat.

"They fight like brothers, and if you spank one of them, they all pout. But they don't need to be micro managed, Tom."

This was exactly why meetings between the old and new regimes were frowned upon. But Tom started it by showing up, so no one could blame *him*, right?

And what if they did? What could they do about it?

"You've done a great job here, Colonel. I have big shoes to fill."

Again with the lump in the throat.

"The key to my success was a lack of attention to memos and paperwork, I assure you. Technically, I'm not smart enough to run a squadron."

Tom narrowed his eyes at him and smiled.

"Yeah, I've heard that, too."

Mac slapped him on the back. "You'll do fine, Tom. Now, any advice on marriage?"

Tom shook his head and laughed.

"None whatsoever, sir. I'm not married."

For the next hour and a half, until Lily returned, Mac shot the breeze with the young colonel, reminiscing about flying and missions and trying to ignore the clawing grief in the pit of his stomach.

Chapter One

Only a fool would miss a party thrown by Chris 'Angel' Gabriel. And Will Pitkin was not a fool.

Gabe went all out. The keg was perfectly chilled, the food was amazing. Music, superb. And since only fools would miss the party, there was always an eclectic mix of people. He had the right digs, too.

If you could find them. You had to weave through downtown looking for an unmarked door wedged between a nondescript boutique and a Hallmark store. Then, if the door was unlocked—it almost always was, but if it wasn't, you had to phone Gabe. Then, up narrow stairs to the landing, Gabe lived in the apartment on the left side of the hallway. He was remodeling the one on the right to rent out. He wasn't independently wealthy like Cruz.

Who called it Gabe's Ivory Tower. Technically, it was a loft. Definitely cool. The place was not especially big. Massive windows ran the length of the front from the shiny stainless steel kitchen to his efficient office. Decor was sparse yet comfortable with strange collectibles scattered about—from vintage swords to a barber pole. Something not quite normal about Gabriel.

Oh, he was a great guy. Funny, hardworking, honorable, loyal, with no end to tenacity or courage, honest to a friggin' fault.

But normal? No.

Even now, at three in the morning, he was set apart.

The others had either left—not before Gabe made damn sure they weren't toasted—or they were crashed here and there throughout the house.

Gabe was the ultimate host. He came to life in a crowd. One on one, he was different. Quiet, almost broody. Awkward. High emotion took a toll on him. Wore on him somehow. Sent him off by himself for days at a time.

He now sat on the couch, with his guitar across his lap, eyes closed, oblivious to those around him. Will watched from across the room. The intricate melody he played seemed effortless. He wasn't lost in concentration from playing. He played because he was lost somewhere inside.

The music gave the darkly lit room a surreal feel, and Will wished he could capture what he saw in words. Gabe was a throwback to heroes of old.

Nic was Batman—a heedless hero who charged in almost before looking.

Hollywood. Well, Cruz was never at a loss for heroism, but he was so over-the-top self-assured that heroism almost seemed a comedown for him. Cruz was not an easy person to explain.

Cowboy. Aw, shucks. What should you say about the kid? Never serious, smart as a whip, best climber Will had ever seen, with a streak of common sense that cut through everyone else's bullshit. If there was one that Will might become best friends with, it was Matt.

The lieutenant. Solid. Unflappable.

Then there was Gabe. He was the Sean Connery version of hero. Polished, though he didn't know it. He could lash out in violence for saying something mean about your mother. But you'd always see it coming if you were watching. Or he'd stop what he was doing to hunt for a stray cat. And, for the last Halloween extravaganza, he arrived in drag.

Girls called him tender and handsome and...

Will's eyes drooped as he listened to Gabe's soft song. If he didn't move, he'd be here for the duration.

He pushed to his feet.

"I'm outta here. Great party."

Gabe looked up as if he hadn't known anyone was still there. He nodded, looked around the room at the others, then nodded again.

"See you tomorrow, Clancy. Glad you had a good time."

Then, he closed his eyes and went back to the song.

And Will slid open the heavy steel door, inhaled the clean, crisp air, and smiled at his good fortune to have friends like these. Even if they did annoy the peewadlin' out of him.

Chapter Two

Chris Gabriel loved the smell of sautéed onions and green peppers. When they were done just right, he poured the eggs into the skillet and swirled it around to coat the sides. In pursuit of the perfect omelet.

A dash of red pepper.

A couple spoons of homemade picante.

Exquisite.

He slid the monstrosity onto a plate, grabbed a fork and lowered himself onto the barstool at his breakfast counter. He gazed out the enormous kitchen windows. Maybe the weatherman would be right. He hoped so, for Julie's sake.

Nic had planned the perfect birthday picnic for them, enlisting the team's help. Cruz was the style king, helping Nic pick out a flawless ring. Though they were engaged, had been for almost a year, Nic was just now springing for a ring. Cruz insisted that Julie needed something to show the world that she really was engaged. Leave it to Cruz to know that.

For today though, Cruz had suggested locations. Clancy added a hint of drama. Cowboy—well he wasn't particularly good for anything except humor in this instance. And Chris had recommended the food: summer fruit, chicken pasta salad, crusty bread, and Julie's favorite brownies.

There weren't many unknown spots in Yosemite, but if anyone knew them, the PJs did. The SAR guys might be the only ones who knew more. This spot was only a short hike, tucked off the path beside an always reliable brook. If Chris remembered correctly, that spot had actually been one of Joey's favorite fishing holes.

Amazing. It had been over a year since Joey died, and sometimes it felt like days. Nic still cleared his throat when Joey's name came up. Cruz suggesting the spot to Nic was, no doubt, not an accident. He could finesse emotion like no one else.

Nic and Julie would go to the park and have a lovely lunch. He'd present her with the tastefully huge diamond, and she wouldn't think a thing of him wanting to go out for beers later so she could show it off. Ideally, she would be surprised by the party.

Savoring a bit, he turned his attention to the comics, starting with Snoopy at the typewriter. He'd save that for Clancy.

Chris spent the afternoon detailing his car. The weather was bright and sunny and far from the wind, rain, and snow of earlier in the week. Indian summer.

The warmth on his shoulders and back felt awesome.

Cruz came by a little after three to bring Julie's card for Chris to sign and put with the gift. He was anal about stuff like that.

"So, Nic's getting laid as we speak."

They both knew better. Nic and Julie were not sleeping together. Cruz's banter was just Cruz being Cruz.

"And you know that how?" Chris asked.

"It's a one-carat diamond. Trust me, Nic's getting laid."

"I'll keep that in mind."

"Right, like you'll ever get married."

"What's that supposed to mean?"

"Nothin'. Just that you're a loner."

Chris didn't reply. Cruz was right, but Chris didn't want to admit it. He'd only thought about getting married once, and it was years ago.

It wasn't a lack of opportunity, really, but a flaw in his personality.

"So, eight tonight, then?"

Cruz chuckled. "Nic's bringing Julie at eight, so maybe seven thirty. Hey, the car looks great."

Chris stirred his Alfredo sauce and glanced at the pasta. With a practiced hand, he drained the fettuccini, threw it on a plate and tossed in the sauce—all in one motion. Then, he perched on his stool, poured a glass of pinot and opened his book. Last night, he'd finished the last Vince Flynn book—taking a moment to mourn Flynn's passing—and now started the newest Brad Thor thriller.

He was thirteen pages in, had helped himself to seconds and had poured another glass of wine when someone banged on his door.

"Who..." he said, distracted as he stood, leaning to finish the paragraph.

The visitor banged again.

"I'm coming," he hollered, again wondering how he could install a peep hole in a sliding steel door. No matter.

At least no matter until he opened the door.

Will sat in the back corner of the Oasis, nursing a beer.

"You're turning my bar into a Chuck E Cheese, Cruz," Fred said from behind the bar. The owner's eyes had gotten big when Cruz brought in the first dozen helium balloons. His face lost all color when Cruz went out to the parking lot and came back in with more.

"It's for Julie," Cruz said back at Fred, as if that explained it.

Will had been there for fifteen minutes before Cruz arrived. It wasn't that he was notoriously early—this time—more that he was out anyway and didn't feel like going home and coming out again. So he was simply early. Now he sat in his favorite spot for writing and watched Cruz tie balloons to the chairs at the tables he'd moved together. Cruz hadn't spotted him yet.

Actually, that statement *had* explained it.

Everyone loved Julie. She was...sweet. Sexy. Sometimes very intense, sometimes playful, but always sweet. Nic was a lucky man. They were perfect for each other.

Those two fit together like the proverbial hand in glove. Her blonde to Nic's dark, but both were top-ten ranked in the *pretty people* category. They'd come in here tonight and mingle with the mere mortals—not that they ever acted like they were above it all.

It was just that they were. Above it all, that is. They were both very friendly, and they'd be all smiles tonight, what with the birthday and the diamond and whatnot. Julie would act surprised even if she wasn't. Nic would laugh and pull her close and everyone in the room would smile and wonder if they'd ever find that perfect love, even if they knew damned well they'd never be that beautiful.

Unless it was Cruz. He and Kit Sheridan could be that beautiful if they ever stopped hating each other long enough to realize that they were crazy about each other.

Will pushed to his feet and wandered over to the table.

"What can I do to help?"

Cruz looked up from the ribbon he was tying and shrugged.

"Get us a pitcher?"

"I got it."

Chris heaved the door open and stood staring. Unable to speak, unable to breathe, unable to move.

"This is a hard place to find," she said, smiling. All dimples and sparkling blue eyes. Her blonde hair was a bit shorter than the last time he saw her, barely grazing her shoulders.

"It's been a long time, Chris."

Suzanne.

Didn't that beat all?

Suzanne.

He backed up so she could come in. She picked up the suitcase beside her and walked inside.

For a moment, he waited, then leaned forward to look out into the hallway.

"No Max?" Chris asked, turning to pull the door closed.

Suz turned to face him. "No Max," she said softly, her eyes never leaving his face. "No Max."

There was a time Chris Gabriel would have given his right arm to hear her say that. Now, her words, and the look on her face, were a knife in his gut.

"What's wrong, Suz?"

She shook her head and stepped forward—all the way—wrapped her arms around his waist and laid her head against his chest.

Chris closed his eyes, breathed her in. Same perfume—*Shalimar*. Same warmth. He could have been in D.C. or at the beach in Grand Cayman.

Time stood still for a moment.

But he wasn't in D.C., and he wasn't in the Caymans, and nothing could turn back the clock. Even if he wanted it to. Which he most assuredly did not.

He opened his eyes and took her shoulders, moving her back a step.

She searched his eyes for a moment, her own filling with tears. Then she turned away and moved toward the kitchen.

"This is some place, Chris. It's you. What smells so good?"

"Fettuccini Alfredo."

"You've already eaten? I was hoping to take you out for dinner."

He reached forward and snagged her elbow.

"What are you doing here, Suzanne?"

She shook her head, stared at the floor for a moment, then looked up and smiled. Seductress red lipstick.

"Is there more fettuccini?"

He let her go. Suz would tell him when she was good and ready and likely not before.

"Sure, come on in."

He poured her a glass of wine and nuked the now room-temperature fettuccini, making his apologies for it not being perfect.

She sat across from him and took a bite.

"It *is* perfect, Chris."

He checked his watch. It was quarter to seven.

"I have somewhere to be at seven thirty, Suz."

"A date?"

"No, a birthday party for a friend. You want to come along?"

"No!"

He reached over and took her hand. The late-afternoon sun streaming in from the windows behind her held her in profile, almost giving her an ethereal look. His gut clenched with concern. And with something more—the instinct to back away slowly. Concern, though, won out.

"What's wrong, Suzanne?"

She sighed, pulled her hand free and took a sip of her wine, then another bite of the pasta. Chris waited.

At last she looked up and spoke. "Please don't tell anyone I'm here."

"I can't..."

"You have to..." She paused, looked away, and took a steadying breath. "Please, Chris, you're the only one I can trust. Please. You have to promise me." She bit her lower lip, maybe a bit too dramatically. Then, without waiting for a response, she looked up and smiled. "Now, go get ready for your party. I'll do the dishes."

When he hesitated, she shooed him away with a flutter of her hand and reached for his book.

"I haven't read this one. Go on."

Chris closed the bedroom door behind him, wishing for the first time ever that it locked, and continued on to the bathroom, which did lock. He showered quickly and then pulled on clean jeans and a black sweater.

When he came out, she was still reading, but she looked up as he neared.

"Wow, you look great. Maybe I should go to beat off all the other women."

What do you say to that? Thanks, but no thanks. Thanks, but your creeping me out? He settled on just thanks.

"Are you staying?"

"If it's okay."

"Sure, there are clean sheets—"

"In the bathroom closet?" The way she said it—all invitation and suggestion—sent shivers through him. Awkward. Like there needed to be so much more said. Like he shouldn't be leaving. "If you go to bed before I get home, you can throw a pillow and blanket on the couch. I'll sleep there."

She smiled as if that matter were up for debate. It wasn't. He snagged his car keys from the coffee table. He was almost to the door when she caught him.

"Don't forget the gift."

He turned. She nodded to the colorfully wrapped gift lying right in plain sight on the counter.

"And Chris," she said as he came back to get the box, "you won't tell?"

"Not tonight."

"No, you have to promise me."

Again, she took his arm. Desperate.

"Fine. I promise."

Chris sat in his car for a good fifteen minutes before starting it up and heading to the Oasis. Had he just promised to lie for her? Christ.

He couldn't remember the last time he was so thrown.

Cancel that, he could remember.

He just didn't want to.

Where the hell was Max? He reached for his phone, but put it back down.

Please, Chris, she'd begged, *don't tell anyone I'm here.* And he'd agreed, for now. That included Max.

The last time he'd talked to Max—must have been around Christmas or New Year's—it was blizzarding in D.C., and they were threatening to close the airports on the Eastern seaboard. Max had said he and Suz were giving serious thought to starting a family. At one time, that would have hurt like hell, but not anymore.

Or so he thought. Until he slid that door open, and there she stood. The one girl Chris had ever loved. And his biggest mistake of all time. His biggest fall from grace.

Why was she here?

Not legal trouble, surely. A JAG lawyer married to a JAG lawyer didn't come to an ex-JAG lawyer for legal help, did she?

She didn't look a day older than the last time he saw her. And that was what? Five—no, six—years ago. If anything, she was hotter. Had he ever fallen for that pout thing she did, though? If she thought that she was going to come here, sans Max, and sleep with Chris, she needed to rethink that plan.

Those weren't the kind of mistakes you made twice. Were they? God, he hoped not.

Chris reached down and turned the key.

Another Saturday night at the Oasis.

Under normal circumstances, it would be busy, provided the PJs were around. When they were on a mission, the place was reputed to be much less so. Tonight Bravo Squad was there in force. No one would miss Julie's birthday if it was in their power to be there. Alpha Squad was represented: Jason, Randy, Steve.

Even though Chris was cutting it close on time, Nic and Julie had not yet arrived. Small favors.

"The present?"

Cruz asked as Chris neared the table, clearly marked with balloons. Cruz and balloons didn't go together. But Julie would love them.

"Cripes." At the irritated look he got, Chris continued, "It's in the car."

The Batmobile pulled into the parking lot as Chris stepped back inside.

"They're here," he announced to the group, setting the box on the table beside a plate of birthday brownies.

He headed to the bar for an ale, trying to force himself to get into it all. He normally didn't have any problem socializing. Tonight, though, his mind was elsewhere, and his insides were twisted.

"You okay, Gabe?"

Clancy sat down next to Chris and fixed him with a curious look.

"Yeah, fine."

"You sure?"

"Yes, Mother."

Chris didn't mean to bark, but everything was definitely not fine, and Chris was already lying. If the strange arrival of Suzanne didn't have him nauseated, the work it took to lie sure as hell did. To top it off, he sucked at it.

In an effort to not further antagonize Clancy—or to provoke his incessant curiosity of all things gossip worthy—Chris pushed back and stood, heading for the lady in the spotlight.

"Dance, Julie?"

She looked up at him and smiled broadly. Since that fateful day at the cabin, she had been very vocal about him being her guardian Angel. It never failed to make him feel good, not that he'd done anything really special to achieve heavenly status.

"I'd love to," she said reaching up to take his proffered hand.

He stopped to appreciate the ring on her hand.

"Isn't it beautiful?"

"Not nearly as beautiful as you, Julie," Chris said, meaning every word. "If Nic is unable to fulfill his reign as king of your heart, I'm sure there will be fight to take his place."

Until the words came out of his mouth, he didn't realize how uncomfortably close his joking was to the tangled mess that had undone the best friendships he'd ever had. And that tightened the knot inside him.

He coughed and tucked her hand into the crook of his arm, walking Julie to the dance floor.

"Even though you're already engaged, hon, congratulations."

She squeezed his hand and looked up.

"Thanks, Angel. And thanks for saving his life for me."

"You're welcome."

It wasn't much after eleven when Chris finished his ale. It was gross room temperature by then.

"I'm taking off," he said, standing up.

That earned him another mother-hen, searching look from Clancy. He just shook his head and moved to the end of the table to tell Nic and Julie goodbye.

Julie was still holding the giant grey teddy bear, the gift from the Bravo guys, which she'd dubbed Abraham, on her lap. Abraham, she said, would keep her company when the team stole Batman away from her.

She stood and pulled Chris down so she could kiss him on the cheek.

"Thanks, Gabe."

Julie turned to Nic, and he waved off the *opportunity* to give Chris a kiss. "Night, Gabe."

Fifteen minutes later, Chris trudged back into the bar. All eyes at the table turned to him.

"Car won't start."

Clancy pushed to his feet fairly quickly, offering to give him a ride. They rode in silence, Chris feeling like he was expected to come clean in exchange for the lift. It was probably just paranoia.

"You ever get finished with that manuscript?"

"Yeah," Chris answered. Clancy was convinced, for no apparent reason, that Chris was just the person to critique his latest novella. It was actually pretty good.

"Good. I'll come up and get it."

Clancy had been bugging him for a week to finished it so he could work on it some more. It took a few seconds for Chris to put Clancy's statement together with what that meant.

"No." Cripes.

"Huh?"

"Not tonight."

Clancy didn't respond, just pulled across empty parking places and stopped. When he did speak, it was pretty much without inflection, and he stared straight ahead. His tone wasn't angry, but careful—measured. "You want me to come get you in the morning, and we'll go try to get your car started?"

"That'd be great. Thanks." Chris tried to sound apologetic.

"I'll call before I come, and I'll honk and wait for you here."

Great to know that he'd pulled off that secret so successfully. Damned if he answered, damned if he didn't. So, he nodded and got out of the car.

As he climbed the stairs, Chris once again wondered if he should call Max. And tell him what? *Your* wife's asleep in *my* bed.

Christ!

Chapter Three

Sunday sunrise found Chris staring bleary-eyed at the ceiling. His eyes burned. He'd never slept on his own couch before. He'd taken the high road a time or two and slept on a woman's couch. He'd slept on plenty of his friends' couches when he was too tanked to drive, but it had been a very long time. And once, he'd slept with a girl on a couch, which, if you could get past the logistics—he was six foot four after all—was fairly awesome.

But, he'd never slept on *his* couch before.

Actually, he hadn't slept on his couch now either, so the record was intact.

He'd come in last night and only the living room lamp was on. The bedroom door, though, was open, and he stood for a moment, looking in. The whole thing was too weird. Just too friggin' weird.

He could hear her breathing as he leaned against the doorjamb.

She wasn't asleep.

He held his breath, hoping against hope that she wouldn't turn over. Wouldn't look at him. Wouldn't invite him in.

Silently, he backed up and headed for the couch.

He'd shed his shoes only to realize that he had to either sleep in his boxers, which really wasn't a particularly wise choice, or in his jeans, which wasn't a particularly comfortable one.

Wisdom won out.

That might have been the reason he hadn't slept.

Right. Who was he kidding?

He hadn't slept because he'd been afraid to.

When he could lie there no longer, he swung his legs down and sat up, running his fingers through his hair. He sat for a time, elbows on knees, head in hands.

He heard Suzanne moving around in the bedroom, and still he sat. Clueless what to do next.

And clueless was one of the worst feelings in the world.

"So, do you still drink Pepsi instead of coffee? I didn't see a coffee pot when I was doing dishes last night. Maybe tucked away in a closet somewhere?"

Chris absently wondered if she was always this perky. He didn't remember her so.

"No coffee pot," he said, finally looking up, the rest of his statement immediately getting stuck in his throat.

She walked toward the kitchen wearing his royal-blue dress shirt. Royal blue to match her eyes, no doubt, and the rest was skin. Very tan, smooth skin. Bare feet.

There was a time when the sight would have sent bolts of heat right through him. Not anymore. Now, it felt presumptuous. Really presumptuous.

He looked at his watch. A bit after seven.

"I'm going to shower. There's instant coffee in the cupboard."

Was that his voice?

Definitely pissy.

He took clothes into the bathroom and locked the door behind him. When he came out, dressed in jeans and a t-shirt, Suzanne was puttering around the kitchen, pouring his Pepsi on ice, toast popping up in the toaster.

"Remember when we used to have French toast with peanut butter on it every Saturday morning?" Pushing a plate of toast toward him when he stalled at the breakfast counter, she smiled. And tipped her head in what looked to Chris like a practiced pose. She still wore his shirt. After she slid his drink over, she came around to sit beside him, sipping a cup of very black coffee.

He did remember. It was in the early days, when he and Max had relented and let her move in to share the cost of their apartment. *Three's Company*—in the JAG office,

19

she was Chrissie, and Max was Jack Tripper because Chris couldn't be. Chris was too practical. He was Janet.

It was also a time when Chris still had the fantasy that Suzanne would someday be his.

"You're looking good, Gabe. Really good."

"Please go get dressed, Suz," Chris replied quietly, not glancing at her.

She let out an irritated huff, sat still for a moment, maybe hoping for a reprieve, then slid off the stool and left the room.

He tossed the toast into the trash, finished his drink, put the toaster away, and rinsed the dishes. Then, he pulled another soda from the fridge and popped the top, pointedly drinking straight from the can—trying to reclaim some autonomy.

Suz took her sweet time showering. When she came out, she wore shorts and a tank-top, more skin showing, her wavy hair still damp. Her makeup was perfect, and her long, dangly earrings actually jingled a bit when she walked. Even a disinterested guy couldn't help notice her breasts puckering beneath the thin fabric. Nothing subtle about her. Chris couldn't imagine how she left this persona behind when she put on a uniform and entered a courtroom.

She paced before the windows for a minute, then walked slowly to where he sat on the couch and lowered herself almost shyly to sit beside him.

"I'm on leave." Her voice was low, nearly a monotone. She pulled her knees to her chest and wrapped her arms around them. "Can I stay here a couple days?"

"Where's Max?"

"In D.C."

A good witness only answers the question you ask, doesn't provide superfluous information upon which the opposing council can pounce. Friends, though, usually didn't do that.

"He's not on leave with you?"

"No."

"You've got to do better than that, Suz."

She flew off the couch, turned on him, hands on hips.

"What do you want from me, Chris?" Her voice was high, nearly hysterical. "You want me to tell you that Max doesn't love me anymore? You want me to tell you that he's lost it? That he's dangerous?"

Now, she whirled and stormed to the window, breathing hard.

Chris moved to stand behind her, careful not to touch her.

"What's going on, Suzanne?" he asked, trying to sound reassuring.

A good thirty seconds ticked by in silence before she moved. Then, she scooted away from him.

"Nothing, Chris. Can I stay, or should I leave?"

His answer was interrupted by his cell phone. "A few days, Suz," he replied, leaning down to pick up the phone from the coffee table. "You can stay a few days."

"So, who's the girl?" Clancy asked as he pulled out of Chris's parking spot in the alley.

"What girl?"

"The girl you've got stashed upstairs."

Chris looked straight ahead. His mouth went dry and his heart sped up. Cruz would laugh at the physical reaction he had to lying.

"No girl, Clancy."

"Whatever," Clancy answered, obviously not convinced. But at least he shut the hell up until they were at the Oasis.

The 'Vette started right off the bat, and Clancy had the decency to not question his assurance that it wouldn't last night.

"Probably a dead spot on the starter," Clancy muttered.

Chris laughed.

"What?"

"You don't know anything about cars. Well-known fact."

Clancy stood up straight and frowned. "Yet here I am..."

"Thank you."

"You're welcome." Clancy tapped the roof of the car. "You okay, Gabe?"

"Yeah," Chris replied, unable to sustain eye contact.

"You sure?"

21

"I said I'm fine. Thanks for the ride. I'll see you tomorrow."

Chris got in his car and, more roughly than he'd intended, slammed it into reverse. When he pulled out of the parking lot, Will was still standing there, watching him leave.

"Something's up with Chris," Will said as he stepped into Cruz's living room.

Eric looked up from the couch. His laptop was open before him on the coffee table. There was a yellow pad beside the computer with Cruz's fancy, girly handwriting on it.

"*Hola. Estoy bien, gracias, e tu?* Eric said, lifting a half-full beer bottle to his lips. He still wore sweat pants and a t-shirt and hadn't shaved.

"Sorry."

"So, Mom, what's up with our little Angel?" Cruz said, again staring at the screen.

"He lied to me."

Will watched Cruz's face as his statement sunk in. His dumbfounded look was chased away by complete disbelief.

"No way. Not Honest Gabe. You're fulla shit."

"No...I'm not. Hide and watch, *amigo*," Will said as he sat down in the easy chair. "So what're you up to?" He reached for the yellow pad and tried to make sense of what he read. On the pad was a list of banks, account numbers, and addresses. He leaned over to pick up the pen he'd knocked to the floor.

"I'm spying," Cruz replied matter-of-factly.

"Really?" Will leaned forward, his interest piqued. "On who—or is it whom?"

"Kit Sheridan."

Will leaned back. Nothing new there. "Why?" he asked with a sigh.

Cruz looked over at him, fixed him with an annoyed look, and then went back to tapping away at the keyboard. "I want to pull a hostile takeover."

"Of Kit?"

"Of her business," he answered, like Will wasn't keeping up.

Will pushed to his feet and turned toward the kitchen. He snagged a beer from the fridge and returned.

"That's a diabolical plan. Why don't you just tell her how you feel?"

"If I could do that, I wouldn't need a diabolical plan."

Chris returned to find Suzanne doing a load of laundry. She'd obviously been *on leave* long enough to have laundry, which reminded Chris...

"How'd you get here, Suz?" For a moment the admonition—never ask a question you don't already know the answer to—flashed through his head. He hated having to be calculating. Downside to being a lawyer—one reason he'd left JAG.

"Huh?"

"Did you fly from D.C., or what?"

She'd been all smiles when he came in. He'd almost expected her to rush into his arms when he first arrived. Now, though, her brows drew together over angry eyes, and her lips flattened out tensely.

"You're as bad as Max with all the questions. If I'm not welcome here, just say so."

Geez.

"I didn't say that, Suz. I was just curious, since there's no car downstairs."

"Did you call him, Chris?"

"Who? Max?"

"Yes."

"No. I told you I wouldn't. Why would I lie?"

"Yeah, really. Why would you lie?" She finished loading her wash into the dryer, slammed the door closed, and pushed the on button. Then, she sidled past him and into the living room.

As he was formulating a coherent response to her overreaction, she whirled around and clapped her hands.

"Let's go somewhere."

What the hell? "Like where?"

"Into the park. Doesn't Yosemite have some pinnacle thing, or something that's famous?"

"Yeah, it does."

Because he couldn't think of a better suggestion, and playing house with her was making him want to slit his wrists, he nodded and let her toss him his keys.

At Suzanne's insistence, they took their food to go. The smell of fries filled the small space in the car.

"Every time I see a red 'Vette, I think of you."

He didn't respond. They drove through the park, mostly in silence. The sun shone brightly. When they neared a spot where they could see El Cap, Chris pulled over, and they got out.

"That's the famous pinnacle thing," he said, laughing.

She took his arm and laid her cheek on his shoulder.

"It's awesome."

He didn't pull away and felt a little silly wanting to. They were, after all, old friends.

"Have you climbed it?" she asked

"On occasion."

She turned to him, lifting her gaze to his face. For a moment, he felt stuck in a much more complicated time.

Finally, she spoke. "Are you glad you made the move from JAG?"

"Most of the time."

"And do you miss me?"

Finally, he was able to pull away. "No, Suz. I don't. You aren't mine to miss."

Cruz sat at the bar next to Will. He pulled out his phone, hit Chris's speed dial, and smiled. Will could see the challenge in his eyes.

"Hey," Cruz said. "Some of us are causing trouble at the O and we're in need of a good lawyer."

As Will watched, Cruz blinked and looked away. "And what's so important that you won't join us?"

Cruz listened, and Will began to gloat.

"Fine. See you at work tomorrow," Cruz said at last, then hung up.

"I told you so."

"He lied to me." Cruz said, slipping his phone back into his pocket. "Something is definitely wrong." Then he grinned and picked up his beer, holding it out for a toast. "We'll beat it out of him tomorrow. Cheers."

Chris sat on the couch, his long legs stretched out before him. Suz sat beside him, not close enough to touch, her bare feet resting on the edge of the coffee table. After explaining the part that PJs played in the *Black Hawk Down* incident, he pushed play on the remote.

He held the phone on his lap, as if his conversation with Cruz could still be redeemed.

In the morning, Suz was asleep in his bed when he needed to get ready for work. With a resigned sigh, he gathered his clothes, snuck into his own bathroom—locked the door—showered and shaved, then snuck back out to the living room. He sat on the couch, pulled on and tied his boots, then grabbed a Pepsi from the fridge and left, a full hour early. Nothing like feeling unwelcome in your own home.

Chapter Four

Chris was trying to sleep in the La-Z-Boy, when the rest of the PJs began trickling in. Alpha Squad's Kevin and Randy showed up first and started in badgering him.

"Hey, Angel. Tough night?"

It never let up. Like a bad contagion, the ribbing and kidding spread. By the time the morning briefing started, Chris had bitten off most of his friends' heads. He grabbed one of the to-dos for the day that would keep him off by himself.

But Cruz and Clancy wouldn't let it go. They trapped him at the meds locker.

"I never thought I'd see the day," Cruz began, leaning against the wall, arms crossed.

"What day?"

"The day Honest Gabe lied to his friends."

Something twisted in his gut, and his grip on his clipboard tightened. What could he say? He stared straight ahead, the labels on the small bottles before him blurring. The whole damned-if-he-answered-damned-if-he-didn't thing was becoming a problem.

"I don't know what you're talking about."

He shut his eyes.

"What the hell's going on, Angel?"

"Nothing. Just..." He paused, trying to control the urge to push his way out of the room, "Leave me alone."

"Whatever," Cruz said and left.

Clancy stalled by the door. "You know you can talk to us, man."

"I know."

Things didn't get any better as the day went on. Even the lieutenant had started giving him searching looks. Maybe he should just call in sick, as if staying home would be better.

There, in his own house, he was a sitting duck. One moment, he was the object of Suzanne's lust, the next the object of her rage and paranoia. Then, he'd spend a sleepless night on the couch and wake to go to work, where he was forced into silence and lies by his promise to her.

When would she just leave?

By Thursday morning, he'd had enough of the whole thing. He hinted at the possibility of her leaving, without any evidence that she'd even noticed. On his way to work he'd even dialed Max, but guilt made him hang up while it was still ringing.

By the time he got off work, he was in no mood to go home and no mood to stay. And Thursday poker, which he couldn't remember ever missing, was iffy. He just wanted to be alone.

When his cell phone rang, and he saw that it was his home phone calling, he just let the call go to voicemail. Then, he deleted the message without listening to it.

And checked into a motel.

Will juggled two pitchers of beer and a stack of glasses as he pushed through the swinging door and made his way to the poker table. For months, they'd been meeting in the back room of the O every Thursday. The mix fluctuated, depending on who was around. But, there were regulars—most of the single guys—and guest appearances by the married ones. Nic, though not technically married, came about half the time. Even the LT showed up every now and then. When he did, he insisted that he be just David, not sir. Kinda like old times, when he wasn't yet a sir.

It had all started one night when they were waiting for a "go" on a mission, and both Alpha and Bravo teams had been sardined into the dayroom watching Texas Hold'em on ESPN. Someone—if memory served it was

Pete from Alpha—suggested that they have their own World Series of Poker. And thus was born the Thursday night game.

They didn't dare play for real money. However they sure as hell kept track and there were *unrelated* payoffs involved. The new TV in the dayroom had come from the hold'em kitty.

Tonight, it looked like seven would be playing.

"Gabe's not coming?" the lieutenant asked.

Will glanced at his watch. After seven. Gabe was normally early.

"He said he was," Cruz answered. His phone rang and he reached into his pocket. "Maybe that's him."

Will watched intently to see if that were the case.

"Yeah, I need to meet with you. Can we do it tomorrow?"

Obviously not Gabe.

"Yup, that should work, I'll let you know if something comes up. I appreciate it."

"No Gabe, then?" Will asked.

"Nope, Kit's paper holder."

"Her what?"

Cruz didn't answer, just grinned and lifted his eyebrows. "*Diabólico, amigo, diabólico.*"

They played until eleven thirty. Gabe never showed up. At nine and again at ten, Cruz pulled out his cell and dialed both Chris' home phone and his cell. Each time, he shook his head.

Chris's pager buzzed its way across the bedside table. The room was completely dark, and for more than a moment, he couldn't figure out where he was. But he instinctively reached for the offending device. The clock glowed red—0347.

The pager code: grab your gear and meet at the hangar. The mission was time sensitive, a life-hanging-in-the-balance thing. Not a search, then.

He pulled on his jeans and sweater, splashed cold water on his face, and tossing the key onto the bed, sprinted to his car.

Both Alpha and Bravo had been called out, and by the time Chris got there, the Black Hawks were firing up.

The last two in were Cruz and Nic. Not stragglers. Just about thirty seconds behind Chris. The teams huddled around for a quick briefing while the helicopters warmed up.

Sometime after midnight, in thick fog and freezing drizzle, a casino shuttle bus plunged off I-80 twenty miles east of Truckee. It wasn't discovered until three thirty.

There were fifty-two people on board.

Airlife helicopters weren't able to get in through the fog. Ground ambulances were headed that way from Reno as were the Truckee fire personnel.

"The bus is down a ravine. Bystanders report some sounds of life, but they can't even see the bus. We've been cleared to land on the highway."

Climbing gear, med supplies, and three boxes of blankets were loaded quickly. The two helicopters took off at 0422. Once in the Black Hawk, their headsets plugged in, they could talk.

"Word of the day, Clancy?" Nic asked.

"Sorry, didn't take time to look on my way out the door."

"Yesterday's then."

"Minotaur—something or someone monstrous, especially one that devours. And the Greek mythological creature, of course."

"Of course. And the day before?"

"Pontificate—to speak in a pompous or dogmatic manner."

"You're a geek."

"Thank you."

Chris interrupted.

"The bus is two hundred feet down. We'll have to rappel."

The group got quiet. Chris continued, reviewing the mass casualty protocol, handing out triage tags as he spoke. It was almost guaranteed that the twin conversation was occurring in the other helicopter.

If they were first on scene, they'd get someone down the cliff to start tagging patients. The walking wounded, who would have to huddle together and stay put since they couldn't climb up unassisted, would get green tags. Dead would get black. Critical patients were red, and those injured severely enough to not be walking around, but not enough to need immediate evac would be yellow.

The real problem, once again, would be communications. Even years after September eleventh, there were still frequency issues. It was possible that the EMS and fire personnel would have a frequency that the PJs' radios had. If not, then the lieutenant would station himself with the scene incident commander and relay information back and forth. Not optimum.

The PJs weren't first on scene after all. The Truckee Fire Department had already sent two firemen down on belay and had some pretty impressive lighting set up on top.

From the gap in the guard rail, Chris could see the mangled bus. It was on its side, laying with the butt end facing the hill and the nose pointing out into the darkness. There wasn't much of a clearing around the bus. A few people moved around, some helping and some wandering dazedly.

"They need some shelter for the walking wounded. Everyone out there will be hypothermic," he said to Nic, who stood beside him.

"And someone to keep them corralled."

"Our thoughts exactly," said a nearby fireman.

Chris had to look at him to see if he really meant that to sound testy. Apparently he hadn't, since the guy nodded with a look of agreement and respect on his face.

It was poor form to sweep onto another organization's scene and take over. Wheels had to be greased, even when there were lives at stake. So, the lieutenant had quickly reported directly to the scene IC and given him a quick idea what the teams could do for him. The teams unloaded gear and waited.

Charis nodded back. "We'll be geared up in three minutes."

"Thanks for coming," the guy said and turned back to the other fireman who was hooking into the line.

"So, we missed you last night, Gabe," Cruz said as he slipped into his climbing harness. "I called you."

Chris shrugged, not looking at him. He peered through the drizzle at the fireman who approached and stepped forward to greet him.

The firemen down at the bus reported bodies everywhere. And a wide variety of injuries. And either the bus had rolled on folks or there were some victims who had wandered off. Initial count only found thirty-eight people.

"Batman and Cowboy on belay."

"At oh-four-forty-eight," the lieutenant's voice answered.

When Chris had first heard that this was a gambling bus, he'd pictured a mix of retirees and just-past-middle-age housewives that normally frequent the casinos, at least on weekdays. But the victims he saw now were younger—much younger—more like in their late twenties, early thirties. No one had said, but this looked to be one of those singles busses radio stations sponsored.

The ground was littered with papers, likely loosed from a briefcase, maybe brought along so its owner could work a bit on the way. They clung to the wet ground where they'd landed. There was a navy-blue high-heeled shoe, and over further, a scattered collection of toiletries.

When both teams were down, they split up. Alpha team worked with the fire guys to set the rigging and begin hauling up those who both had a chance of survival and needed immediate evac on the waiting Black Hawks. They'd rigged for multiple patients, and each Black Hawk would take one PJ. Other patients would be triaged and treatment started inside the warmth and dry of the waiting ground ambulances. The moderately injured would be taken, two at a time by ambulance, to Reno.

That left Bravo to search the perimeter of the crumpled bus for victims who, in their confusion and pain, had wandered off.

As the sun broke the far-off horizon, the light filtered through the fog, giving the entire scene an out-of-body feel to it. Chris glanced up the hill, watching Kevin and Randy, one on each side of the Stokes litter, being winched up the hillside. Soon, it disappeared into the mist. Except for the muffled sound of the rotors of the Black Hawks, it was as if the resources at the top of the cliff weren't even there.

The drizzle had let up some, leaving a hanging sogginess in the air. Chris zoned back in to hear Nic and

Cruz arguing over which of the two Bravo teams would get Cowboy. Matt was definitely the best tracker from either team, having spent his childhood years hunting with his dad in the wilds of Colorado and his teen years working summers as an outfitter.

If he hadn't felt so disconnected from everyone around him, Chris would have smiled.

He hadn't smiled in a very long time. And that really felt odd. He wasn't given to this oppressive heaviness that seemed to overwhelm him.

He stood alone a moment longer, then sprinted to catch up with Cruz.

Together, they headed clockwise around the perimeter from the back of the bus—six o'clock—and Cowboy, Clancy and Batman went counterclockwise. They'd meet in the middle at the front of the bus—or twelve o'clock. It wasn't particularly scientific, but it had been Wiley's terminology and, for working a perimeter, it seemed efficient enough. They radioed the plan to the lieutenant waiting up there somewhere.

"Sir, Hollywood and Angel going off clock at about the eight thirty spot."

One didn't need an expert tracker to follow a blood trail into the darkened forest, where they were forced to pull out their flashlights to stay on target. Footprints indicated only one subject.

"There," Cruz said pointing forward, and began jogging in that direction. Chris followed, keying his mic as he went.

"We've got one subject ahead, sir. Standby for details."

It was a man. His right leg was covered with blood and he lay face down in the sagebrush and pine needles. Chris watched as Cruz crouched down and reached check for a pulse, closing his eyes as if actually listening.

Seconds ticked by, Cruz intent.

At last, he looked up at Chris and shook his head.

"Sir," Chris said quietly, "we have one deceased male here, guessing mid-forties." Then to Cruz, "ID?"

Cruz checked the man's slacks, found the wallet, then spoke. "We have ID, sir. This is Paul Winston, born March seventeen, address in Citrus Heights."

There was a brief pause while the lieutenant checked the passenger list. "Marking Paul Winston deceased. Please relay your coordinates and check the perimeter for any sign of others."

Chris and Cruz didn't find any more stragglers, but the other Bravo guys did. A gaggle of them. Five wanderers, all now in various stages of shock, hypothermia, and two that needed to be evac'd right away.

"Angel, you guys go help Batman's team."

Chris looked at Cruz and received Cruz's best "duh" shrug. As soon as they'd heard the other team's report, they'd headed, too, in that direction.

"Way ahead of you, Lieutenant," Chris answered, smiling at Cruz. It felt good.

Cruz smiled back.

Nic's voice broke in. "Angel, we need boards for two of these. Can you bring them with?"

"Got it."

They detoured back to the bottom of the hill, glanced around for a stash of unused backboards—to no avail—and radioed up top. Before the boards arrived, though, one of the fire guys brought them two. "We're not quite ready in there."

The guy nodded to a newly cut hole in the bus.

"How many inside?" Chris asked.

"Three dead, three iffy."

"Thanks. If we get back in time, we'll come help."

"No problem. One of your other guys is still in there."

That meant that the other Alpha members were likely on the helicopters. Something to be said for that—he envied them. At least they were out of the elements.

With the light had come—only the light. If it had gotten any warmer and less soggy, you couldn't tell it.

Chris didn't envy those working in the bus itself. Cramped quarters were hard to maneuver in. When movement was further limited by the care you had to take with a patient's spine, it was even worse. Being tall didn't help, either. But the fact remained that, if they were done before the guys in the bus, Chris and Cruz were there. No questions. No hesitation.

It was after eight in the morning when the last of the yellow-tagged patients was hoisted up the incline, long since turned to mud. In dry conditions, they'd have had everyone up the hill in an hour. But despite being roped in up top, the hill was so slippery that, at one point, it had been debated whether crampons would help—not that they'd brought crampons with them. They were stored with the ice climbing gear.

By nine, all the survivors were loaded and on the way to care. Everyone, with the exception of the lieutenant and the fire captain, was covered with a thick coating of drying mud, adding an additional ten pounds to what each one carried. Firefighters began shedding their turnout coats, and PJs began peeling off layers. Then, substantially lighter, they began coiling ropes and gathering gear.

The fire guys would haul up the bodies, but not until after the feds and the coroner had finished their work.

Chris glanced at his watch, fully expecting it to be after noon—it was only ten forty. It felt like they'd been there days. He was hungry and thirsty. As soon as the helicopters returned, they'd be able to get out of there, eat, and hit the showers before the gear cleanup began.

"Hey, guys. We have some food and Gatorade over there." The speaker was a girl. He hadn't noticed before, but now that he looked around, he saw several females amongst the fire personnel.

"Thanks," Cruz and Clancy spoke in unison, their voices suddenly taking on a well-rested quality. They shot each other a scathing look, then Cruz stepped forward. "I'm Hollywood, this is Clancy." Then he nodded toward Chris, "And Angel. Over there are Cowboy—the little one— and Batman."

The girl grinned, but more in fun than appreciation. Then she held out her hand.

"Wonder Woman. But the offer stands."

Food sounded good, but the Gatorade sounded better. Chris followed Cruz and Clancy to the back of one of the fire trucks, where the food and drink had been laid out on the ground. Neatly wrapped sandwiches, all marked with their ingredients, apples and strawberries, a package of Oreos, and another of Chips Ahoy.

The PJs joined the firefighters sitting in the middle of the closed highway. No one talked, everyone too busy feeding. At last, someone leaned back against the wheel of the fire truck and belched contentedly. Scattered laughter followed. It was good to wind down.

Chris knew, though, the minute that he saw Quillen approach, that the plan would change.

Chapter Five

The LT looked from one of his guys to the next, his gaze finally falling on Nic. "We have two unaccounted for," he said quietly, then paused so their tired brains could process the information. "They may be under the bus." Then he stopped talking and looked down at the ground before him.

Lt. David Quillen was the best leader Chris ever had. He stated the facts, and more often than not, allowed his men to come up with the action plan.

"They may not be," Nic said for them all. "How long 'til we have the bus moved and know for sure?"

The lieutenant glanced over at the fire captain for the answer.

The captain checked his watch. "Maybe forty-five minutes 'til the crane gets here. I honestly don't know how long it will take once it's here. It's pretty far down there."

"Don't we know it," one of the firefighters answered.

"Sir, I'd like us to start a search, just in case," Chris said.

Even the firefighters, to a man—or woman—nodded.

The captain turned now to Quillen. "You're more versed in search than we are, Lieutenant. You make the call, and I'll leave it up to my people if they want to join in. That is, if you want our help."

So much for getting a warm shower. A sandwich was better than nothing, but real food would have been nice. Not that Chris was ungrateful.

"Captain, thanks for the food," Chris said aloud.

"You're welcome. I'll pass on your thanks to the Ladies Auxiliary. If you're going to search," he paused and glanced again at Quillen, who nodded, "I'll have them put together something hot for when you come out."

The teams began to unroll the rope again and repacked for what they'd need in the field. Fourteen of the twenty firefighters stayed, mostly the volunteers. The paid staff had to get back to cover town.

Search plan established, the PJs divided into five teams, each taking a few fire personnel with them. Shockingly, Wonder Woman ended up on a team with Cruz and Clancy. Chris and Nic had two guys and one girl on their Team Three.

The missing were twenty-eight-year-old Jerry Murphy, dark hair, five foot eleven, one hundred eighty-five pounds, and twenty-seven-year-old Mike Francis, dark hair, five foot six, one hundred sixty pounds, glasses. All info was from the DMV.

The teams were nearly two miles out, searching in lines radiating from the bus, when the radio confirmed that the two missing men were, indeed, under the bus. One was dead. The other still had a pulse and was immediately loaded onto one of the Black Hawks. The teams turned and trudged their way back through the thick forest toward the bus and the promised hot meal.

This time, the wrapping of ropes and stowing of gear dragged, even after they'd eaten—buckets of fried chicken that they could smell—or at least thought they could—from down by the bus. The early call out, being wet and cold for the entire day, dragging mud around for hours, all added up to drain their energy away. That, and the reality that they wouldn't be done for the day until all the gear was ready to go again.

Idly, while dragging sloppy, heavy rope up the hill, Gabe remembered having the same conversation with Daniel Fraser, the civilian SAR captain. He'd struggled to convince his teams that they couldn't go home immediately upon returning to base. It had taken, if Chris remembered correctly, some fairly severe consequences to get the guys to finish the job before they left. At the moment, though, going home to his bed sounded pretty damn good.

The thought lodged in his head, and he grimaced at the reality that he'd have to kick Suzanne out or he was either stuck with the couch for the foreseeable future. Damn it all.

In order to allow the highway to reopen, the Black Hawks ventured to the closest town to perch as the crew waited for the teams to finish up. At Quillen's word, they reappeared, drawing an excited crowd of gawkers from the cars stopped for the landing.

By the time the helicopters had reached cruising altitude, Chris was nearly asleep, trained as they all were to take combat naps where and when they could. Nic actually had to be shaken awake by Quillen when they touched down.

Climbers neglect their rope at their own peril. Or so the poster on the wall in the big room of the Section said. At the moment, none of them particularly cared, but they also knew they *needed* to care.

When ropes got muddy, and you ran ascenders or even prussic cord along them, the grit was forced into the microscopic fibers that held each of their lives in the balance. Under normal conditions, ropes were carefully inspected after each mission—a slow, time-consuming job. But now, they had to be washed first.

So, outside they trudged. They hosed the ropes down, then pulled them through the rope washers until the water ran clean. The ropes were hung from biners suspended from the ceiling and allowed to air dry.

None of this, though, until they'd showered and started the three washers with their coats and fleece and whatever else they could stuff in there.

It was after eleven when they headed to their cars.

The friggin' 'Vette wouldn't start.

Chris laid his head against the steering wheel, closed his eyes, and tried again. Nothing but the tell-tale clicking Clancy had warned him about.

"Damn it all."

Fine. He'd sleep here, in the La-Z-Boy. That is, if he could move from the spot. Maybe he'd just sleep in the car.

Tapping at his passenger window forced him to look up.

"C'mon. I'll give you a ride," Clancy said with a tired smile.

Chris reached for the door handle and unfolded himself from the car.

"Thanks."

"No problem. But this time, I'm getting that manuscript."

"Whatever."

Main Street—downtown Merced—was pretty much deserted this time at night, except for the patrons of the martini bar down the street. Still, they were able to pull up right in front of the street entrance to the loft. Chris dragged himself from drowsiness and got out, grabbing his duffel bag and hefting it to his shoulder. His biceps screamed with the action. By morning, his whole body would be sore. It didn't matter that they were all in great shape—they had to be—when you overused muscles, they let you know.

It wasn't until he slid the key in the lock of the street entrance that he remembered the problem with Clancy coming up. He stopped dead, and Clancy sighed.

"I'll stay in the hall."

Chris didn't reply and they both trudged up the stairs to the second floor foyer to the two loft apartments. His on the left, and the one he was remodeling on the right.

When he got to his door, Chris froze again.

"I said I'd stay out here," Will said.

Chris took a step back and paused to look over at Clancy. Clancy glanced at him, then at the door. It was open an inch. Chris quietly lowered the duffel to the floor and carefully pushed the door open.

Dark inside and their eyes were acclimated to the light in the hallway. Chris peered straight in toward the living room and saw nothing out of place. He reached in and flipped on the light and again paused for any response from inside.

Still nothing.

He stepped in.

Just inside, the hallway opened to the left, into the TV room that, in turn, opened into the kitchen. The TV room was fine, nothing out of place. But as his gaze continued on, through the next doorway into the kitchen, everything was definitely not fine.

"Jesus Christ," Clancy said behind him.

Chris flew to the body that lay sprawled on the floor.

"Oh, shit."

It was Max.

Dead. Blood on his chest. Pooled on the rug. "Suzanne!"

Chris sprinted through the house, circling through the kitchen, through the living room and into the front office area that led to the bedroom.

He flipped on the bedroom light and stood for a moment, trying to make sense of what he saw. Or didn't see.

Suzanne was not here.

The bed was neatly made. Her things were gone.

Chris felt a warm rush of relief that she wasn't lying in a pool of blood herself. That was followed all too quickly by cold dread.

His heart in his throat, he made his way back to the body, now more and more aware of the stench of death.

A gun lay in Max's dead grip.

However, Chris knew beyond question that Max had not killed himself. He also knew that if ever there was a time to come clean, this was it.

But how could he do that? He'd promised to keep silent. Besides, she might be in danger too. He'd keep her secret for a bit longer.

Clancy fixed puzzled eyes on him as he neared.

"Gabe..."

"You need to leave."

Clancy started to shake his head.

"I mean it, Will. Leave now."

The look he gave Clancy must have been vicious because the determined expression faded, chased away by something akin to fear. Clancy took a step back, then hesitated. With another glace at the body, he turned and headed for the door.

"And Clancy," Gabe words caught him as he reached to pull the heavy slider closed, "you didn't come up with me. You just dropped me off."

Now Clancy's face closed down altogether but he

nodded before he disappeared from sight.

Chapter Six

Only eight hundred meters into her morning swim, Claire Janova sprang from the pool, snagging a towel with one hand and her ringing phone with the other. Her ring tone was a cheery Yankee Doodle Dandy. She was anything but. When you worked out this early, especially on a Saturday morning, you should never be interrupted by the danged phone.

"Janova,"

"C.J., you up?" The gruff voice of the JAG commander stopped her, breathing hard.

"Yes, sir, up and running—so to speak."

"How quick can you get in here?"

"Uh, an hour?"

"Sooner if you can."

"What's up, sir?"

"Max is dead."

"Be right there."

It was quicker to pull her hair up than to French braid it which she normally did. Max Delati, dead. Wow. The office would be in a frenzy of gossip and supposition and even lawyerly stuff like who, and how, and why. Did Suzanne know? Did Suzanne care? Did Suzanne kill him? Banish the thought.

Claire slipped into her shoes and picked up her purse and briefcase. Then, she headed down the stairs to the garage. Normally, it took her twenty minutes to make the drive. This morning—this early—it took only thirteen.

She pulled her clunker Chevy up to the guard shack and returned the crisp salute of the smirking guard. She imagined that hers was the worst car ever to carry an officer sticker at JAG headquarters, maybe in all the Air Force. But she had better things to spend money on. After Greece last spring, she was shooting for Japan next. Having the guards smirk was worth the eventual payoff. She'd send them a postcard.

She dropped her things at her desk and made her way to the commander's office. His clerk wasn't in yet.

"Sir," she said, knocking on his door, "it's Janova."

"Claire, come in."

Colonel Grisham stood at his sideboard and glanced at her over his shoulder.

"Coffee?"

"Please," she replied, sliding into one of the two chairs that faced his desk.

He returned and handed her a steaming mug.

"Thanks." She glanced at the contents and smiled politely, despite the fact that she preferred cream and sugar. "So...Max?"

"Right. I got the call just before I called you."

"From whom?"

"Police in Merced, California."

"Wow, they were up late." Six a.m. here was three in California. "What happened?"

Grisham frowned and leaned back in his chair, bringing his own mug to his lips as if he were trying to warm himself. Colonel Grisham was a good commander, as far as Claire could tell. He was tolerably friendly without being pushy or nosey and let his people do their jobs. The only time he butted in was when there was a clear problem or when he was invited to. He really trusted his people, or he didn't have the energy for both work and the tumultuous goings-on with his teenage daughter. Claire wasn't really in on the office gossip pipeline, but one could not miss the tension when the girl stomped through the office.

"The initial report is suicide."

"Max? Really? How?"

"Gunshot to the chest. He was at Chris Gabriel's house."

"Who?"

The colonel slid a folder across the desk to her. She opened the file and scanned the information inside.

"Former JAG, huh? Here?"

"Yes. He, Max, and Suzanne all worked here together before Chris jumped ship, so to speak, to become a PJ."

"So Lieutenant Gabriel is now Sergeant Gabriel." She stopped before the next words—"that's dumb"—came out of her mouth. What kind of an idiot gave up a hard-earned commission—for anything, much less to be a jock?

"Right. I guess Max left here Thursday morning. I heard about it late in the day. Some sort of emergency leave."

Claire finished reading through the page in the folder and waited. She had a ton of questions, but knew when to hold off and let the answers come to her.

"I want you to fly to California."

"Me, sir?"

"Yes. You've only been here a month. My guess is that you're not given to gossip and that you'll be the cleanest slate I can send there, pardon the mixed metaphor."

"Okay. And what is it you want me to do?"

"Well, I want you to find out what happened. Discreetly, of course. Without getting in the local's way, if possible. You seem to have a flair for investigation and criminal law, so have at it."

Claire was home just after seven, before the D.C. traffic got horrendous.

She had copies of three work files, one each for Max, Suzanne, and for this Chris Gabriel. The Colonel assured her that he would pave the way for her as much as possible with the Merced P.D. and with the 506th Rescue Squadron's new commander, Colonel Tom Scott.

With Grisham's blessing, she'd wear civilian clothes—jeans, in fact.

"You'll be working off the books, so to speak," he'd told her. "But take a uniform just in case. I don't think anyone will question someone from our office asking questions about one of our people's death. If you have problems, don't hesitate to call me."

"I won't, sir, but I don't expect problems, either."

Claire didn't expect problems. She'd never had problems getting what she wanted or needed. Historically, some folks credited that on having a mother in the Colorado state legislature. She knew that others thought she got by on her looks. Really, her looks had, at times, been a handicap. The truth was, though, that she just had always had a way with people. They seemed to want to help her.

Ideally, she would arrive in Merced, hit the police department, and they'd share all that they had with her. Then, she could move on to check out whatever questions their information raised.

Chris didn't know how long he'd been sitting at the kitchen counter. Long enough that his legs were numb. Actually, he was pretty much numb all over. He'd probably slept sitting up, despite the fact that officers, some in uniform and some in street clothes, had been in and out of his apartment all night.

One in particular, a Detective Jim something-or-other, maybe thirty-five—built like a bulldog, wearing jeans and a sweatshirt—had asked him questions from time to time, his face completely expressionless, not bothering to take notes.

The consensus at this point was that Max had offed himself. When Chris noticed how casually the cops had said it, they'd half-heartedly begged his pardon. Bulldog now stood across the island from him, telling him that he'd be best served to find a motel room and get some sleep.

"We're going to be here a while."

"Did someone call Max's commander?"

"Yes, our chief did hours ago."

"And his folks?"

"I don't know."

"I'll call them," Chris said. It would be better coming from a member of Max's extended family. There was a time that Chris called Mr. and Mrs. Delati Mom and Dad. But that made it no easier. Chris was so bad at the emotional-entanglement stuff.

"Fine, then find some place to sleep, Sarge."

"Right."

The desk clerk watched him get out of a taxi and didn't ask why he was checking in again.

Chris didn't elaborate. He didn't sleep, either.

It was an unwritten rule in the real world, Chris supposed. The phone ringing between midnight and seven in the morning meant only one thing—bad news. Of course, for the rescue business, it meant the same thing, but just not *your* bad news.

"Mr. Delati, Chris Gabriel." The stone wedged in the pit of his stomach since approaching his door last night turned over.

The line was quiet for a few very long beats.

"Is he dead, Chris?"

"Yes, sir."

"Where?"

Where, but not how? That was mind boggling. So was the fact that he didn't even act surprised.

"Merced, California, sir."

"California?" Mr. Delati paused as if taking in the information. But he didn't ask any of the natural questions—why was he there, how did he die. "I need to tell his mother. Thank you for calling, Chris."

The call ended abruptly, leaving Chris even more unsettled. It was like Max's father had been expecting it.

Chris pushed to his feet. His cell rang again before he slid it into his pocket. Caller ID said Clancy. He glanced at his watch. It was just after four in the morning.

"Hello."

"Anything I can do?"

Clancy wasn't usually so to-the-point.

Chris needed to get his car.

"Can you come get me and take me to my car, maybe jump it if it won't start?"

"Sure."

"Now?" Chris wanted to get in and out of the base parking lot before everyone arrived. Besides, he had to find Suzanne, sooner rather than later.

"I'll be there in ten."

Before Chris could say thanks, the call disconnected. It wasn't until after he'd hung up that he realized that it was Saturday, and there was no real rush to get the car.

True to his word, Clancy pulled up out front at four twenty. He was quiet all the way into work, to Chris's utter relief. But it didn't last.

"You need help with this, Angel." They pulled into the empty parking lot and parked on the driver's side of the 'Vette.

"No, I don't, Clancy. But I do need you to refrain from running your mouth." Chris was immediately sorry for the way it came out, but left it at that. Clancy said nothing else, just waited to make sure that the car started. When it did, he just saluted and drove away.

"Damn," Chris muttered under his breath.

He slammed his baby into gear, apologized for doing so, and made his way off base and back to the motel. He'd sleep for a few minutes and then come up with a search plan.

By noon, Claire was on a United flight out of BWI to Fresno, where a rental car waited for the hour drive to Merced. She'd change planes in Denver. The entire day would be eaten up with the trip. At least she'd gain three hours as she went from east to west.

She had time to begin sorting out her thoughts and putting together a plan. The three files lay on her lap, and she idly flipped through them, stopping at the personnel picture of Sergeant Gabriel.

The man was classically handsome and was smiling for this picture, his eyes crinkling a bit at the corners. He had short dark hair and gray eyes. His file said he stood six foot four inches tall and, if the weight listed was accurate, he was lanky.

But what really boggled her mind—still—was that he'd given up a career in law and his officer rank to play hero. His letter said that he wanted something more hands-on, something more physical. He'd also written that, of late, he'd "become disenchanted with a legal process that wasn't particularly interested in truth." Claire understood, but it was up to the individual to force the truth into the light. The system couldn't do that for you.

It was only months after Gabriel left JAG before Max and Suzanne married. Suzanne kept her name, and the two of them managed to stay stationed together in D.C. What little scuttlebutt Claire had overheard said that Max and Suz were going through some rough times.

Apparently, they'd both been TDY to Iraq for a case, and Suzanne had ended up in a building that came under enemy fire. She'd returned changed—disturbed or something—and had been on medical leave a good bit since.

Her file barely mentioned this medical leave, except for one letter from a psychiatrist officially requesting a meeting with Grisham.

Claire jotted a note to ask the colonel about this meeting. Legally, he could tell her little, but maybe he'd fudge a bit.

Sipping her Coke, Claire's thoughts returned to Sergeant Hero. Why did his career choice bug her so much? What difference did it make to her that he'd thrown away his college degree and his future? Claire Janova wasn't a snob.

She was practical.

Not a snob.

Chris woke to the ringing of his phone. In the darkened room, curtains tightly shut, he was forced to look at the clock to get his bearings. He reached for the phone as he cursed himself. It was after ten in the morning.

"Care to fill me in, Sergeant?"

It was DQ, and he was pissed. Chris got to his feet, an automatic response to rank.

"There's nothing to say, sir. An old friend came to visit me and ended up killing himself on my living room floor."

"That's your story, Gabriel?"

What had the lieutenant heard? What had Will told him? Damn. "That is the story, sir." This whole thing was spinning out of control, and he was helpless to stop it. He'd given his word. Damn. Damn. Damn. That made lying no easier. DQ measured his words.

"Okay, then. If I can do anything, let me know."

"Thanks, sir."

"Stay in touch, Chris."

"Right."

Chris showered and got dressed in the clean clothes the cops had allowed him to bring—only after searching through them. What he really needed was Hollywood. Cruz could get on his laptop and find out where Suz was. He'd use some borderline illegal technique from his days in Intelligence and in minutes Chris would have his answer.

Maybe.

That wasn't possible at this point. Chris wasn't about to implicate Suz in Max's death. Suicide. But damned if he didn't wish he at least had her cell phone number.

Maybe he should call Washington.

Like he could do that without tipping his hand.

This sucked.

It sucked a lot more for Max.

By the time Claire pulled into Merced, there wasn't time to stop at the motel. She'd called the JAG assistant from Denver and had her make reservations in Merced. Claire's only requirement was a pool where she could do her laps in the morning.

But for now, she headed straight to the Merced P.D. to touch base with them.

Before getting out of the car, she ran a brush through her hair and pulled it back into a clip, then finger applied some lip gloss. She blinked into the rear-view mirror, wished herself luck and grabbed her purse.

It took exactly twelve minutes to be ushered into the office of lead detective Jim Medina. Apparently, a murder in this sleepy town kept everyone working, even on the weekend. From the looks of the tiny office—one desk, one chair—he might have been the only detective. He didn't seem pleased to meet her, but was tolerably civil. At her introduction, his eyes widened, and he half smiled.

"You're the JAG lawyer?"

She pulled her thoughts back in line and played the game.

"Yes, Jim, that's me. I just got in from D.C. and was really hoping that you could fill me in on the death of my co-worker."

"Max Delati?"

"Right."

"And I was hoping that you could fill *me* in on *him*."

"I'd be glad to tell you what I can. I'm rather new in D.C. So I didn't know Max well."

Jim Medina's smile faded back into what looked to be a perpetual frown, complete with jowls. His stance was set, unyielding and facts did not come from him easily. But Claire had learned early on to read upside down. She gleaned a bit from the file he had opened on his desk. She was even able to see the top photo of Max. The sight made her stomach lurch.

Small-town detectives were notorious for being inept. What she saw didn't contradict that, and certainly did not compute with the official story. Unless there was something she was missing—and that was entirely possible—Max Delati did not commit suicide.

Chapter Seven

Chris took a chance and dialed the JAG office in D.C. He was routed to a clerk that sounded like he was thirteen-years-old. Perfect.

"Listen, Airman," Chris said, doing on his best irate JAG officer impersonation, "This is Captain Ritchey from Eglin and I'm fed up with the run-around. You either help me, son, or..."

"Yes, sir, I'll do my best, sir."

Excellent.

"Airman, I need a cell number for Suzanne Johannsen ASAP."

"Sir, I—"

"Don't sir me, son. Just give me the number. Or give me your commanding officer's number. Right now."

"Yes, sir. One moment, sir."

Cruz woulda done it with more flair. Woulda made up some huge whopper with intricate details.

But, Chris got the number. Once he hung up though, he realized the danger of calling from his cell and walked across the street to use the archaic pay phone attached to the throw-back cafe.

For the last four hours, he'd dialed that number every thirty minutes. To no avail. He left message after message begging her to call his cell. He'd chance the trace to be able to talk to her.

Beyond that, he didn't have a clue where to look.

He called her parents in Arizona, reminding them who he was and telling their voicemail that he'd lost her number and was looking to get hold of her and Max. He said he'd call back.

And now he sat in a back booth and waited, searching his befuddled brain for another idea. When the waitress passed, he flagged her down for more Pepsi.

"Well, sir, the detective wasn't exactly forthcoming with information, I'm afraid."

"You need me to go over his head?"

"Not yet." Claire didn't have enough information to draw a good conclusion, but she wasn't ready to admit defeat. Despite her certainty that Max had not pulled the trigger, she had no facts. Gut feeling wasn't reliable. She trusted logic. "Let me see what I can dig up tomorrow. I'll call if I need help."

Grisham okayed her plan, trusting her to do her job. Good.

She needed to get her hands on that file, on the photos, on the reports from the scene, and when it came in, the autopsy report.

From the police department, she drove to the Gabriel apartment, hoping there'd still be cops there and she could talk her way in. It took a few times around the block to put together that Sergeant Hero lived above a charming little boutique that was now closed. The door on street level—unmarked and unlocked—led up to a small hallway with two heavy steel doors marked "A" and "B." She knocked on both—stung her knuckles—but no one answered.

She contented herself to find the Best Western on Motel Drive—imaginative name that was.

At eight thirty Saturday night, Chris got the okay to go back to his apartment. Bulldog stiffly reminded him that he'd probably have a few more questions for Chris tomorrow and for Chris to stay available.

"Whatever, Detective," Chris said before hanging up. He checked out of the motel room, paying for a night he wouldn't spend there.

Then he drove home.

Home to a house that felt foreign.

Home to bloodstains on the beige rug that went through to the wood floor beneath.

Home to a bedroom where Shalimar still lingered in the sheets.

By Sunday morning, he'd lugged the bloody rug out of the house, into the apartment next door for now, used ammonia and water to get the blood up from the floor, laundered the sheets on the bed, and snoozed for thirty-five minutes on the couch.

At eight thirty, he pulled his fourteenth Pepsi—but who was counting—from the fridge and rushed to answer the door, hoping against hope that it would be Suz.

Sergeant Gabriel was clearly expecting someone else when he pulled open the door. His expression went from anticipation to disappointment to no emotion whatsoever in a matter of seconds.

Claire looked up into pearl grey eyes and held out her hand.

"Sergeant Gabriel, I'm Claire Janova."

He peered from her hand to her face and back to her hand, but didn't move a muscle.

"I'm a JAG attorney from D.C."

Still, nothing.

"Can I come in and talk to you?"

Chris was rooted to the spot. He'd been hoping—expecting—the woman on the other side of the door to be small and blonde, not tall and dark. And gorgeous. She wore jeans, sandals, and a crisp striped blouse. Her dark hair hung down past her shoulders. She had a voice that struck him first as hoarse, but then as acutely sultry.

A JAG attorney from Washington?

Grudgingly, he found his manners—he really didn't want to see anyone aside from Suzanne—and a JAG attorney was low on the list. But good breeding was hard to overcome. He reached out and shook her hand, impressed by her firm grip.

"May I come in?" she asked again, smiling.

Smile or no smile, this woman was all business. And while she didn't, at this point, appear threatening or sinister, he was wary. But he had nothing to hide.

Freudian slip.

He had a great deal to hide, just none of it because he, personally, was guilty of anything.

Except maybe stupidity.

He stepped back. "Come in."

Sergeant Hero reluctantly let her inside. For a strikingly handsome man, he looked like hell.

"When was the last time you slept, Sergeant?" she asked, actually shocking herself. The way he straightened his shoulders told her she'd shocked him as well.

"What do you want, Lieutenant?"

"Actually, it's captain, but call me Claire. I'm here unofficially by request of Colonel Grisham to find out what happened to Max." As she spoke, she wandered inside to what looked to be a living room.

The apartment had beautiful wood floors and walls made from glass block, giving the entire space a lot of light. The living room was straight in and was lined with near-floor to ceiling windows that looked out at the second-floor apartments across the street.

Turning left, just past the couch that faced the fireplace, she saw a pool table, and beyond that, a very modern-looking kitchen. Gabriel had followed her. He now stood looking out the windows by the pool table, absently twisting the ring on his finger.

"Grisham, huh?" Gabriel said.

"You know him?"

"Yes."

"So, Sergeant, you want to tell me what happened to Max?"

The question was interrogatory, the tone was light. Chris winced anyway.

"The police deemed it suicide."

"Did they?"

"That's what they told me, before kicking me out of my own house."

"Is that what you think? That Max committed suicide?"

"I don't know what to think."

The way the light played on her dark hair was a bit distracting. But when she turned and smiled, full-on, showing dimples that went with the slight cleft in her chin, Chris began to wonder if he'd lost his friggin' mind. His body reacted, and he had to concentrate to keep up.

"You found Max?"

"Yes."

"Why was he here, Sergeant?"

The way she used his rank made him nervous, irritated.

"You can call me Chris."

"Why was he here, Chris?"

"I don't know. He showed up while I was on a mission. I didn't know he *was* here."

"So the first you knew of it was when you found him dead?"

"Yes, *Captain*."

Claire smiled. The witness was becoming hostile. Time to switch tactics.

"I'm sorry. I know this must be hard for you. I understand that you and Max went way back."

Tired or not, grieving or not, Chris Gabriel was not stupid. Now he smiled at her, but not in a good way.

"Listen, Captain, I don't know what happened here, and I'm not in the mood to play your games. Besides, I've got things to do." He held out his hand pointing the way out. "If you have questions, maybe you should ask the police, and leave me alone."

Her cue to leave.

"Thanks for your time," she said, hoping it didn't sound like a line—she did mean it. She moved past him and toward the door, only stopping when he moved to open it for her. "One more quick question, though. Have you seen Max's wife recently?"

He whipped around, the door halfway open. "What's that supposed to mean?"

"Nothing. She's been missing for over a week. We're concerned."

"Goodbye, Captain Janova."

"Bye, Chris."

Chris listened to Janova's steps fade down the hall, then he turned and walked through the TV room, coming to stop at the spot he'd spent most of the night scrubbing.

The blood stain was no longer visible, but it would never be gone.

He crouched down and ran his fingers along the floor.

"I'm sorry, Max."

If he hadn't called Max and hung up, maybe...

Chris squeezed his eyes closed on the emotion that surged into his throat. He pushed it away and rose.

How in hell was he going to find Suzanne?

"You're hiding something, Hero," Claire said to herself as she pulled the car door closed. "You certainly reacted to my mentioning Suzanne, didn't you? But I just don't think you're a killer."

She slid the car into reverse and pulled out of her parking space, heading toward the base in hopes of talking to some of the people who worked with Gabriel. Being a Sunday, she might or might not be successful. Maybe she'd at least get some phone numbers.

Chris punched the gas and flew around a slower car, taking the exit that led to a lesser known entrance to Yosemite. He'd thought getting out of the house would help. Earlier, he'd tried the cafe across the street and ordered breakfast. But when it showed up, his stomach clamped down at the thought of eating. He stabbed at the sloppy eggs and, after one bite of bacon, pushed the plate away.

Then, he'd phoned Suzanne's cell again from the pay phone with the same results. What was it they said about insanity?

But he had finally gotten ahold of her parents, trying hard not to tip his hand. Her mom informed him that Suzanne had disappeared from D.C. ten days ago, cleaning out her bank account. The D.C. police called this morning to tell them that Max had been found dead in California. Suicide, they'd said.

Mrs. Johannsen's voice cracked then, and her husband took the phone from her.

"Chris, let us know if you hear from her, please."

"I will, Mr. Johannsen."

Apparently, they didn't know that Chris was the one who found Max. He didn't enlighten them. He also didn't ask how much money they thought she had taken from the bank or if she was in her car or... He just couldn't get his brain to form logical questions or his mouth to ask them.

Driving hadn't helped, either.

Maybe scenery would.

Or not, since the stranglehold on his throat had nothing to do with where he was or what he was doing.

The PJ building loomed over the nearly empty parking lot. Claire followed the Jolly Green Giant footprints to the front door and entered beneath the outstretched wings of the pararescue angel. The only one in the building was precisely the person she was looking for.

David Quillen was friendly, if a bit cautious. He also knew nothing that she didn't already know, but was fiercely protective of his Angel.

Angel? Claire rolled her eyes.

But the image of Sergeant Hero was starting to soften a bit.

"Gabe is one of the good guys, Captain. And he's as honest as they come."

Claire was dubious and must have broadcast that somehow because Quillen angled his head and looked at her intently for a moment. Then he leaned over his desk and jotted down names and numbers. He handed her the slip of paper.

"You don't believe me, fine. Ask the guys he works with."

Maybe it was California. She was totally striking out. Every time at the plate.

Claire had never been to California before and at this point, she wasn't sure she wanted to come back. She must have left her mojo back in D.C. because she was off-kilter somehow. People weren't reacting to her the way she was used to. This Gabriel guy saw right through her, and apparently, so did his lieutenant. The detective hadn't helped her much, either.

She glanced at the names on the paper: Eric Cruz, Nic D'Onofrio, Will Pitkin, Matt Wiley. Maybe she'd get somewhere with these guys.

"Thank you, Lieutenant."

"You're welcome." He handed her his business card. "Call me if you need anything else."

Maybe she misjudged him.

"Thanks. I will," she said, reaching to shake his hand.

He took hers in a warm, firm grasp and paused, his eyes sharply fixed on hers. "And you'll keep me in the loop."

"Of course."

She stopped at a convenience store for coffee. Before going in, she pulled her tablet from her purse and logged in to her connection. Quillen had given her names, but nothing more. Within minutes, she had addresses for Cruz and D'Onofrio. They apparently shared a place. She had Pitkin's as well. For some reason, Wiley's wasn't listed. If she still needed it later, she could call the personnel office to get it.

She filled her travel cup with a machine cappuccino—her one real vice—and headed for the two-birds-with-one-stone address, pulling up just as a dark-haired man and a pretty blonde girl came out.

"Can I help you?" the man said.

"D'Onofrio, or Cruz?" she asked.

"D'Onofrio. And you are?"

"Claire Janova, JAG."

"JAG?" he asked hesitantly. The blonde looked over at her guy, concerned.

"Yeah, officially unofficial. I'm here checking into the death of a co-worker."

The look on his face—wow, this guy was nice looking—told Claire that he was completely lost in this conversation.

"Apparently, my co-worker was found dead by your Sergeant Gabriel?"

"Angel? Really? When was that?"

"Friday night."

"First I've heard of it. What do you need from me?" He reached over and took the girl's hand.

"Can I just ask a few questions about Gabriel?"

"You think Angel killed him?" The girl stepped forward, straightening up as she spoke.

She was a Gabriel defender, big time.

"No, nothing like that. I'm just gathering information. I assure you..."

"Please, ma'am, come on in." With that, D'Onofrio steered his sweetie around and led the way into the house. "By the way, this is my fiancée, Julie Galloway."

Julie only nodded, still guarded.

"A pleasure, Julie."

Eric Cruz was inside. He was quintessential beach boy, wearing shorts that said *Chick Magnet* and a bright yellow muscle shirt.

"Eric, this is..." D'Onofrio paused, shrugged, and continued, "...Claire Janova, she's JAG."

The same guarded look crossed Eric's face before he grinned and reached for her hand.

"Captain."

Good guesser, or he'd spoken with his Lieutenant.

"Eric."

"She's here to ask about Angel," Julie informed him.

"Sure, Claire. Ask away."

Okay, this guy was smooth—first addressing her with rank, and then casually switching to her first name. And since he didn't ask why she was there, she was pretty sure he'd talked to Quillen, probably just now since he hadn't had a chance to fill in D'Onofrio.

"Have a seat. Can I get you anything? Coffee, soda, a Corona?"

D'Onofrio tossed his friend a confused look but then sat down, drawing Julie down beside him.

"No, thanks. I just hoped you guys could tell me about Gabriel."

Before she could get anywhere, Will Pitkin showed up. Cruz introduced him to her, and though cordial, Will was clearly uncomfortable.

"So, tell me about this Angel of yours," she reminded them.

Cruz sat forward. "Sure, he's great. Trustworthy, honest, honorable..."

"He's a champion," Julie interrupted quietly. "A true champion."

All eyes went to Julie. D'Onofrio squeezed her hand. Cruz smiled. Will nodded.

"He's a knight in shining armor," she continued. "He's loyal and..." She stopped and gazed at D'Onofrio, her voice husky with emotion. She looked back to Claire and smiled. "You can trust him."

The room was pin-drop silent when she finished. Apparently, there was little that needed to be said.

Claire let it hang there a moment, then turned to Pitkin.

"So, Will, had you heard about Gabriel finding his friend dead?"

"Yes. Well, no. Well, yes. I talked to Yoda this morning."

"Yoda?"

"Lieutenant Quillen," Cruz filled in, giving Will a look that Claire took as warning.

"Oh." She asked Will. "But you haven't talked to Gabriel?"

"No, ma'am."

It seemed that Sergeant Hero—make that Sergeant Champion—had good friends who would defend him fiercely. The Chris Gabriel she'd met hadn't appeared to fit what his friends said about him. And despite the differences, Claire found herself wanting to believe the hype.

She reached into her hip pocket and pulled out a business card.

"Listen, guys, if you think of anything that I might need to know, please give me a call on my cell phone. I'm staying at the Best Western here in town."

She stood up, and the guys followed suit. Julie stood as well.

"Look, I'm not the enemy here. I'm just here to find out what happened to Max. I'm not out to get your friend."

When none of them answered, she cut her loses and left. Hunger rumbled her stomach, so she drove through Burger King and got food, then let her frustration take her back to the motel where she changed into her suit and ate **by the pool**.

Chapter Eight

"So, Clancy, what do you *really* know?" Nic turned on Will as soon as the captain pulled out of the driveway.

"Nothing more than you do." Will might not be Honest Gabe, but he wasn't all that good at lying, either. Besides, he always knew more than anyone else about anything that was going on.

"Okay, this sucks." Cruz headed to the kitchen and came back with a Corona. "Gabe's in trouble, Clancy, and you'd best come clean."

"He's not in trouble, Cruz."

"What part of that last conversation did you miss? There's a JAG lawyer sniffing around. Gabe finds his one-time rival dead in his apartment, and he's not in trouble?"

"Rival?"

Julie let out a little squeak, then shut her mouth tight.

Nic cleared his throat, and Cruz sat down, taking a long draw on his beer. Will looked from one to the other, then sat down himself.

"Do tell."

Now Cruz laughed, "Ooh, something that we know that Will Pitkin doesn't. It's a long, sad tale, Clancy. Suffice it to say Max got the girl Gabe wanted, and our boy Gabe had a slight fall from grace in the end."

This was the first Will had heard of this story. He needed more. "Details, please. Need to know."

Cruz glared at him, measuring the *need to know*. Then he looked at Nic, who shrugged.

"C'mon, you guys."

"Once upon a time..."

Will blew out his frustration, and Cruz grinned.

"...our erstwhile hero, Angel, and his best friend Max lived in harmony as JAG attorneys in our nation's capital."

No use getting his panties in a wad. Cruz would be Cruz, no matter what.

"The cost of living was such that they wanted a third roommate, and the Lady Suzanne filled the bill."

Suzanne. The name Gabe had called when he found Max's body.

"Gabe, Max, and Suzanne were the best of friends. But Gabe loved her from afar. Since he was loath to say anything and wasn't into relationships—you know our Gabe—he said nothing and ignored his feelings. Max didn't. Soon, Max and Suzanne were a couple, and Gabe, always loyal to a fault, quit loving the girl."

Nic snorted at the last statement. Julie sat forward, as enthralled by the story as Will was.

"One night, when Max was out of town, one thing led to another, and nature took its course. Suz begged Gabe not to tell Max. He never did, but he swore he'd never lie again. And so was created the Honest Gabe that we all know today. Within a week, he turned in his resignation from JAG corps and put the wheels into motion to join the PJs."

It took a moment for Will to shake free of the story and for reality to sink in.

"That's not true," Will said, pushing to his feet.

"Yeah, it is." Nic said in Cruz's defense. Cruz, for his part, took another sip of beer.

"Wow. That's out of character."

"Yup," Cruz held up the empty bottle. "This one's empty. Fetch me another."

Will did what Cruz demanded, not because he was obliged to but because he was up, and he wanted one as well.

"Nic? Julie?"

"Nah, we're good."

The group was quiet for a time, all pondering the facts. Julie broke the silence. "Do you think Claire knows that story?"

Will nearly choked, sat up, and caught his breath. He looked to Cruz, then to Nic. "God, I hope not."

Julie flew to her feet. "Angel didn't do it. I know he didn't."

"They said it was suicide," Cruz said. Nic took her hand and pulled her back down beside him.

"Then why was she asking all those questions?"

Again, looks of concern went around the room.

"I don't know, Julie," Cruz answered. "But we'd better find out." With that he pushed to his feet, downed his beer, and went into the kitchen. When he came back out, he had his keys in hand.

"Who's with me?"

"Where?"

"To see Angel."

"I'm in," Will said. He had to go, had to somehow convince Gabe he hadn't said anything and had to do it without saying anything else.

"Um," Nic said.

Julie jumped in. "You go. I'll head home. You should go."

"I'm in. Thanks, babe."

They took Will's car since it had enough room and was parked in the driveway.

Coming out of the park, Chris stopped for gas and another Pepsi. Despite the amount of caffeine he'd had, he still felt dull. Maybe it was the humidity. It had been threatening to rain since he got up, never quite getting there.

He stopped at a convenience store and—wonder of wonders—they still had a pay phone too. So he put in one more call to Suz's phone, which still accepted messages. That meant she had heard the earlier ones.

And hadn't called him back.

He left another plea for her to call him, then pushed away from the booth and headed to the car.

Then he headed home.

Will's car was parked in the alley when Chris pulled in. But it was too late to turn around. He stopped shy of the parking spot and waited for Will to back up so he could pull in. But, the doors opened at that point and Cruz and Nic got out, walking toward him.

"Damn it, Clancy," he muttered out loud.

Will had blabbed and now the entire team was out to help him. Just what he needed.

Damn Clancy.

In what he knew would get his ass kicked once they caught up to him, he threw the 'Vette into reverse and hurled dirt up getting the hell out of there.

Seconds later, his phone rang. He didn't answer. He knew who it was and what they'd say.

And he didn't need their help.

Not much, anyway.

Will watched the 'Vette back away, knowing he might never convince Gabe that he hadn't talked. By the time Cruz and Nic got back to the car, Cruz had already dialed his phone. He climbed into the passenger seat cursing. Then he dialed again.

"Lieutenant? You at work, sir?"

DQ worked way too much. He needed some sort of life. That was funny. No one gave Clancy credit for having a life, either.

But he did. Kinda.

"We'll be right there. We need to talk."

Cruz slid his phone into his pocket and nodded to Will. No one spoke again until they walked into the Section.

"What's up boys?" DQ said from his office, even before they made it down the hall. Then he stepped out and steered them into the dayroom.

"Sir, Gabriel's in trouble."

Will stood back and let Cruz take the lead. Better to watch the lieutenant's face and less chance he'd be called upon to lie again.

The lieutenant nodded. "Go on."

Will was somewhat surprised to hear Cruz tell the Gabe-Max-Suzanne story to Yoda. Usually, he'd have held his cards closer to his chest. Either he was extremely worried about Chris—hell, they all were—or he trusted Yoda on this one. Not that Yoda wasn't trustworthy. He absolutely was. But he was their boss and you didn't rat to the boss under normal circumstances.

These were anything but normal circumstances, though, weren't they?

When Cruz finished the saga, DQ said nothing. Just sat, breathing, staring over Cruz's head.

"Do you think Gabe killed Max?" the lieutenant asked.

"No."

"What do you think?"

True to form, DQ was not quick to offer his two cents. Much more willing to let his men work through things themselves first. DQ was a good leader.

"I think he's in trouble, sir. He's lying to us and avoiding us, and that's not like him. I have a hunch that he's in deeper than he knows."

"And what is it you want me to do?"

It wasn't a challenge. It was an honest question, more from a friend than from a boss.

"Talk to him. See if he'll open up to you. I don't know, sir."

DQ sat for a bit longer, then stood. "I'll do what I can."

"Thanks, sir."

"No guarantees, Eric."

"I know. Thanks."

Claire's luck was turning. Detective Medina wasn't in this evening. And the guy spoke to was young and had practically tripped over himself when she walked in.

He introduced himself as Dennis Hannigan, completely ignoring all rank or even that he was an officer.

"What can I do for you Miss Janova?"

Better to leave it at Miss as long as things were going well.

"I was hoping to get a copy of the Max Delati case file, Dennis. I'm here from Washington, investigating his death."

Vague. Vague was good. Let the guy think whatever he wanted to.

"Oh, well, let's see..."

The kid struggled for only a moment before dashing back to Medina's office and returning with said file. He chatted away happily about his aunt, who used to live in Virginia "somewhere or other near the Capitol" while he copied every scrap of paper in the file. Then with a did-I-do-good twinkle in his eyes, he handed her the copies and boldly asked if she'd had dinner.

"I have, yes. Perhaps another time, Dennis. Thank you so much."

Then she pivoted gently and fled the building before someone caught her pulling her hand from the cookie jar.

Not exactly comfortable going to a restaurant for dinner. Merced was not very big. Murphy's Law would send Dennis Hannigan to whichever restaurant she went to, and she'd be caught in a lie. Claire snuck through the drive-thru under the Golden Arches and headed to the motel.

Once in the safety of her room, she flipped on Headline News to catch up on any important happenings in the world. Then, she kicked off her sandals and spread out the food and the file on the bed.

The list of questions grew with every turn of the page.

The number one question wasn't for Chris Gabriel, either. It was for Detective Medina. The photos of Max's body clearly showed and almost perfect circular powder burn surrounding the hole in his chest. Hard to achieve turning the gun on yourself.

How, in the name of *Law and Order* and all things holy, did the local yokels arrive at the conclusion that Max Delati committed suicide?

Chapter Nine

Claire was up and swimming laps before the sun rose. It wasn't the first time she'd had to charm a maintenance guy to let her into a pool this early. Swimming in the dark was stimulating in an odd way. There was just you and the water and the lamp at each end of the pool. It gave you time to think, time to order your steps for the day, time to come up with a plan. Her plan for the day was to corner Julie Galloway's champion and get some answers.

The last time Chris felt this crappy about going to work was when he was still with JAG. It was a bad time in his life. Things had gone to hell with Suz and Max, but it was more than that.

Some people he prosecuted were clearly innocent, and some he defended were clearly guilty. The politics in the JAG office moved from simply irritating to unbearable. And, for the first time in his life, Chris was lonely.

He never minded being alone. But being alone in a house with people who were his best friends, being alone in an office he'd worked in for three years and most of all, being alone in wondering why the hell he was doing what he was doing started to get to him.

So he jumped ship. A friend from the Academy had just become commander of a rescue unit. First, Cary encouraged Chris to become a PJ, then he helped him get slotted for school.

Chris never looked back.

And he loved this job. It wasn't a job, it was an adventure. Hoo-yah.

Until today.

He reached for the phone and dialed the lieutenant's cell phone.

"Quillen."

"Lieutenant, this is Gabriel."

"What can I do for you, Sergeant?"

A little more clipped than Yoda's usual.

"I need a personal day, sir."

"No."

Chris hadn't expected that answer. But beyond that, he hadn't expected it to come without any consideration whatsoever. It was like DQ had expected his call.

"Sir?"

"I want you in my office at 0800."

Chris was quiet. He wanted to argue. He wanted to cuss.

"Sergeant?" DQ pressed.

"0800. Yes, sir."

The line went dead in Chris's hand.

The Champ's red 'Vette was pulling out of the other end of the alley as Claire pulled in. She followed discreetly. Before long, though, it was obvious where he was going.

Not optimum, but what had been? Okay, that wasn't exactly fair. She had gotten her hands on the case file. But if Dennis the Menace told his boss what he'd done, there was likely a coming storm from Medina.

Welcome to California, Claire.

She kept going straight when Gabriel pulled into the Section parking lot and took the scenic route back around, driving past the two Black Hawks that stood ready for the next mission. Then, once in the parking lot, she reviewed the file again, giving him time to come back out if he were only stopping in for a minute. She much preferred having this conversation one-on-one, with no witnesses. She had a hunch Gabriel would, too.

A few of the Alpha Squad guys were in already. No Bravos, though. Chris checked his watch. Ten 'til eight.

"Mornin', Angel." A chorus of *hellos* from the dayroom.

So, Clancy hadn't blabbed to anyone besides his closest friends. The day was young. Damned Clancy.

"Gabriel."

Yoda never yelled. Chris couldn't think of a time he'd ever heard him raise his voice in anger. Actually, if anything DQ got quieter when he was angry. Then, it was time to run the hell away. Or so everyone said, though Chris wasn't entirely sure anyone had ever tested the theory. DQ ran his teams with a subtlety that kept big problems at bay.

His voice was serious, but that was all. Still, a flash of warning surged through Chris, sending waves of apprehension through his gut.

"Come in, Gabe, and close the door."

Randy was passing in the hall and stopped at DQ's words, fixing Chris with a *you're-going-to-the-principal's-office* look. Chris didn't take the bait, just straightened his shoulders and continued.

"Sit down, Chris."

He didn't argue. DQ already sat, and pushed aside the papers he was shuffling. But he didn't look up.

"Your teammates are concerned, Chris."

Chris didn't know what to say to that. If he asked "about what?" he'd be dissing both his team and his lieutenant. So he said nothing and tried not to shrug.

DQ looked up. "You're not a liar, Chris."

God, his mouth felt like it was filled with sand.

"I assume you have a good reason to do so now?"

"I hope so, sir."

Claire had given him enough time. She glanced in the mirror out, then got out of the car. And found herself walking into the building with Eric Cruz.

"Captain," he said as he held the door for her.

"Thank you, Sergeant."

"*De nada.*"

She let Cruz pass, then continued on down the hall, coming up short when Cruz stopped to talk.

"What's going on, guys?"

"Gabe's in with Yoda."

"And?"

"And it's too friggin' quiet in there."

When said speaker caught sight of Claire, he turned three shades of red and muttered a "Beg your pardon." And when Eric, God love him, introduced her as Captain Janova, said speaker jumped to attention.

Claire waved him off. "As you were, Airman. I'm not here as a captain."

"Still sorry, ma'am."

"Apology accepted."

She turned to Cruz. "So, what do you suppose your lieutenant is talking to your champion about?"

"Your guess is as good as mine, ma'am," he replied, then sauntered off down the hall. Claire was stuck for the moment. She tried to stay as unobtrusive as possible for a woman in an all-men's club. Soon, Will Pitkin showed up with another kid, whose name tag verified that this was Matt Wiley.

"Can I help you, ma'am?" Matt asked before receiving a warning look from Will. But his boyish grin remained, and he totally ignored his friend.

"I'm waiting to speak with Sgt. Gabriel."

"Angel," the kid hollered and was immediately shushed by the guys hanging in the dayroom.

"In with Yoda. Door closed. Shut up."

"Sorry, ma'am. It seems Angel is indisposed at the moment."

"So it seems."

Their conversation was cut short when the front door opened and Detective Medina sauntered in, accompanied by two uniformed cops and one MP.

"Chris, I really want to be able to help you here. So do your friends. But as long as you remain mute, there's little we *can* do for you. If you'd tell me..."

DQ stopped. Sighed. Looked away.

Chris's throat ached, and his eyes burned. He sucked air in small, quick breaths, trying to control the emotion that surged from his chest.

This man was someone Gabe trusted—*could trust*. He trusted his team, yes. But, the lieutenant was more than a friend, though friend he definitely was.

Maybe he could let down his guard.

Maybe he could allow the LT to ease the pressure he felt, even for just a few minutes.

Maybe he could come clean.

"Sir, I..."

His throat closed on the words, and he was only able to lay his head in his hands and breathe.

Yoda waited silently.

The phone ringing in his pocket made Chris jump, and he reached for it before considering.

It was Suzanne.

His heart raced at the sight of her number. He glanced up at Quillen, knowing that his face was unguarded as he did so.

Chris stood up, wanting to flee, wanting to answer the phone.

Quillen said nothing, but shook his head.

The moment had passed.

Then, he looked past Chris and stood quickly, completely in tune with the pulse of the building. Things outside the office had gone calm-before-the-storm silent.

With a smothered curse, Chris slid the still ringing phone into his pocket. When the lieutenant pulled open the door, Chris followed him out.

They didn't get far. DQ, though a good five inches shorter than Chris, stood between the approaching storm and his PJ, even if Chris hadn't leveled with him. The lieutenant would go to the wall for him, no matter what.

"Let them through, sir," Chris said quietly.

DQ slowly turned, fixing Chris with earnest concern.

"It's okay, sir. I've done nothing illegal."

He couldn't say he'd done nothing wrong because he had. He'd lied to most of the people he cared about and some he didn't. He hadn't given false testimony to the cops—hell, that was a felony—but he had held back the whole story.

"I believe you, Chris."

"Thank you, sir."

When DQ moved aside, Medina stepped forward. By now, they had drawn a crowd. Eric stood behind Chris as did Jason and Pete. Behind Medina stood Cowboy and Clancy. And with them, damn it all, was Claire Janova.

"Chris Gabriel, I have a warrant for your arrest for the murder of Max Delati."

Complete silence, as if the room held its breath while the detective read Chris his rights and one of the officers stepped behind him with cuffs.

Even though he was innocent, at that moment he felt like someone had punched him. It was a feeling like no other, and for an instant, he thought he might cry. He sure as hell couldn't speak.

"You might want to find yourself a lawyer, Sergeant."

"I *am* a lawyer, Detective," he managed before Claire Janova stepped forward.

"And he has an attorney. I will be representing him."

"Really," Medina said, his voice thick with sarcasm.

"Yes, really."

"Isn't that interesting?" Medina smirked before steering Chris down the hall.

"You know the drill, Gabriel," Claire said from behind him. "I'll be there shortly."

Claire fought the urge to follow as she watched them walk away. For an instant, she was stuck between being an attorney, who'd watched clients cuffed and led away countless times and something else. That something else made her clear her throat even as she questioned her sanity.

The bottom line, though, was that she knew as surely she'd ever known that her new client was not guilty. She'd been wrong on occasion, but she wasn't now.

"Captain."

She turned to see Cruz standing behind her. She blushed as if he'd caught her somewhere she wasn't supposed to be.

"He'll need bond money. I'll be down shortly with whatever is needed."

"Cruz, it will be a while before you can do that. They'll need to arraign him first. Give me your number, and I'll call you when I know more."

"God," he said, scrubbing his hand over his face, "this is a nightmare."

"Yeah, it is." In more ways than one.

"You believe him?" Will asked from beside her.

"He lied to me," she replied.

Will, Cruz, and the lieutenant all looked at the floor.

"For the record, aside from the lie, he hasn't told me enough to give me any indication of his guilt or innocence," Claire continued. "He mostly saw me as the enemy, I think. Besides, I could ask you the same thing. Do you believe him, Cruz?"

"I believe *in* him."

"All right then," she said, shrugging. "Let the games begin."

There were times when the Section was eerily quiet.

When someone got hurt.

When someone died.

And, apparently, when someone got arrested for murder.

"Cruz, my office," DQ said and Cruz turned to follow closing the door behind them.

"Can you find out who called Gabe's cell phone a few minutes ago?" Quillen asked.

Eric couldn't remember DQ ever sounding so desperate, so urgent—even in the midst of a mission. He was clearly out of his element here and grabbing for help where it could be found.

"I don't think so." But, at the look the LT gave him, he changed his answer. "Yes."

"Then do it."

Will stood in the hallway for a good five minutes watching the door Angel had gone out. Six-foot-four Angel, one of the most honorable men he knew, led out in cuffs. The world had simply stopped making sense.

The war inside him began in earnest. It was one thing keeping information from his team when there was nothing at stake. It was quite another now.

They couldn't believe Gabe killed that guy, could they?

Dumb question. Clearly, they could. And did. On top of that, they'd have to have some actual evidence, or at least some damned-good circumstantial stuff.

The crowd had cleared. The Alpha guys were back in the dayroom. Nic and Cowboy had wandered back toward the locker room. And, after Cruz emerged from the LT's office, the lieutenant left the building, headed for the commander's office.

They'd arrested Gabe.

How was that possible?

For murder!

His muddled meanderings and the dead quiet were interrupted by a shout from the dayroom.

"Clancy, what the hell is going on?"

It was Kevin from Alpha. And usually, Clancy was the right one to ask. He was the most likely to know everything happening in the Section and in the Squadron.

And he did know—at least more than they did—but he was sworn to silence.

This sucked.

Without answering, Will escaped out the back door.

Chris had never even wondered what it would feel like—cuffed and folded into the back of a squad car. Never considered it.

His knees were smashed against the seat in front, and he sat forward so the cuffs wouldn't dig in any more than they already were. That brought his chin almost to his knees and left him fighting the claustrophobia that threatened to choke him.

The back seat was hard plastic—presumably so it could be hosed down when people puked—not impossible even for him. Every turn left Chris sliding with no way to catch himself. Had they done that on purpose, to keep you humbled? It worked.

He shut his eyes.

Breathe in.

Breathe out.

The distinctive ring of his cell phone made his eyes fly open. The officers had confiscated it—along with everything he had in his jumpsuit pockets—and put it in a plastic bag that now sat between the two officers in the front seat.

Chris held his breath, hoping they wouldn't pick it up, willing Suzanne to end the call.

If it was her.

What did it matter, anyway?

It would take all of a few minutes, or so Cruz had told him, to get the listing of everyone who'd called him and everyone he'd called.

Oh, God.

And he thought things were spinning out of control before.

Chapter Ten

The police station was only three blocks from his loft, yet it was an eternity away. If someone had asked him a month ago how he would feel were he arrested for murder, he likely would have laughed it off and told them that: A, it would never happen and B, if it did, he was an attorney, had been *in jail* lots of times and that he'd stay professional.

He wasn't laughing now.

And he felt anything but professional.

He felt stupid and scared and wished more than anything to see a friendly face. He'd never been one of those guys who saw the cops in an adversarial light. Couldn't remember ever calling them *pigs*. Well, maybe once or twice in high school when they broke up perfectly good partying on the beach. And while Medina hadn't been exactly polite, he hadn't been nasty. Except that look he'd given Claire, which pissed off Chris big time. But now, even though both uniforms were extremely polite, they felt like the enemy.

How many times had he advised potential defendants that once you were a suspect, the police were not your friends? Ask for your lawyer and shut the hell up.

Aside from the horror of being handcuffed, sliding around in the back of the cop car, and now allowing himself—like he had a choice—to be thoroughly searched and fingerprinted, he also felt humiliated.

The only thing that would have been worse than being arrested at work, in front of the only real friends he had—and Claire Janova—was if Julie had been there. She seemed to think he walked on water and disappointing her would have been unbearable. Who was he kidding? Just because she hadn't witnessed his finest moment didn't mean that she wasn't disappointed.

"Right hand, Sarge," the booking officer said, holding out his hand to take Chris's.

They'd taken to calling him Sarge with an air of familiarity. The better to eat you, my dear. Soon, they'd be slapping him on the back like they were old friends, telling him that, if he's innocent, he'll do better just talking to them, and then offering him some sort of deal for his cooperation.

And while Chris didn't particularly want to see his lawyer—what was that telling them she was his lawyer stuff about anyway?—he would go through it all with the few words he would permit himself to say: I want my lawyer.

The thought almost made him smile. Cruz would have made some utterly sexist, X-rated remark at this point that was chock-full of double entendre. On the other hand, thinking about Cruz brought a lump to his throat.

He swallowed hard, squeezed his eyes shut for a moment, and pushed all emotion firmly away. He would get through this. He would.

It could take up to six hours for booking in the big city, but Claire figured Merced might be different. She'd allow two, then go in there and demand to see her client. By then, they'd be done with the paperwork, the fingerprinting and the inevitable we're-here-to-help-you interview. Thank God, Chris knew better.

Now, if he'd just start acting in his own best interest.

With a new sense of herself—she'd suddenly gone from casually here to investigate a murder—to here on a very professional mission—she headed back to her car, walking with a little more purpose. Or so it felt.

First, she'd go back to her room and change into her uniform—good thing she'd brought it—then, she'd find a pancake place near the police department. It was something of a tradition, going way back to the days in Colorado when she'd spent hours studying at the Village

Inn near her home. She'd done it ever since, especially when she really needed to concentrate. Weird, yes, but it worked.

She needed to look at the files with fresh eyes.

She needed to call the boss and get his blessing on her new job.

And, she needed to put on her official persona.

All that, while she ate French toast with strawberries and whipped cream. God, she loved this job.

Eric Cruz stood in the lieutenant's office with the door closed for the second time today—and it was only nine thirty. It had taken more time to get the piece-o-shite printer to *print* the list than it had to *get* the list.

It helped to know the back alleys of the web. At times like this, he didn't regret the time he'd spent in intelligence. He'd gotten out because it frustrated the snot out of him to sell the higher ups on his ideas. That and the old technologies. He could do more now, with his smart phone and his knowledge than he'd ever done in that old position. Never mind that he wasn't actually *supposed* to be doing it.

"I have the list, sir." In his hand, he held the list of numbers Chris had called and those that had called him over the last week. He'd also traced a select few. Yoda didn't reach for the list, so Eric just held onto it.

"Who called him while he was in my office?"

God, he didn't want to answer. He didn't want to answer even more than he hadn't wanted to do this in the first place. When he'd balked—by mistakenly trying to convince the lieutenant that he *couldn't* get the list—Yoda had stared him down 'til he relented.

"Cruz?"

"The phone is listed to Suzanne Johannsen."

Yoda closed his eyes and let out his breath. His reaction was similar to Eric's when he'd chased the rabbit to that end.

"Sit down, Eric."

It was the first time in well over a year that Eric saw that look in David's eyes. DQ had been just one of them, one of the PJs, for many years. He was squad leader, yes, but still, one of them. But then, he'd gone away to OTC and come back a lieutenant. From time to time he still hung with them, watched TV in the dayroom. But now, he carried responsibilities.

Real responsibilities.

He was a great officer, had always been a great leader.

But at the moment, he was just David, wanting to have a conversation with Eric. Cruz sat down.

"What do you think?" David asked.

"Can you tell me about the phone call?"

David considered for a moment, then spoke with a sigh. "I got the feeling he was ready to tell me what was really going on—wanted desperately to tell me. But his phone rang. He didn't answer it, just looked at the caller ID. Then, he clammed up. He did say he hadn't done anything *illegal*."

"He's measuring his words."

"Yes, he is."

"He's in trouble, sir. Deep trouble."

"Yeah."

David sat, absorbed, for a few minutes.

Cruz waited.

"Eric, off the record. See what you can find."

"Okay." Eric got to his feet and had the door half open when David spoke again.

"Is Will acting strangely?"

Cruz hadn't really noticed. "Maybe, now that you mention it."

"Send him in, will you?"

"Yes, sir."

"Thanks, Eric."

Will knew the moment Cruz pulled him from the supply room that his day was shot to hell. Of course, he had zero room to complain.

"You wanted to see me, sir?"

DQ sat at his desk, with only one file folder before him. It was the cleanest Will had ever seen that desk.

"Yeah, Clancy. Come in, and shut the door."

An ominous sign. Will couldn't remember the last time Yoda had closed his door. Maybe two months ago, when Wiley broke his thumb showing off on the mechanical bull down at Rowdy's. Today, he'd lost count.

Will entered, shut the door quietly behind him, and stood at attention before the lieutenant.

"Relax, Will."

"Right, sir," Will answered and moved to a modified parade rest. He had the sudden urge to wipe his hands on his thighs. Ick.

"Sit."

Will sat.

"Traditionally, you're the one that knows everything going on around here, Will. So how come this time you aren't?"

Will couldn't look up. He'd always thought he could lie with the best of them—well, maybe not like Cruz, until now. But suddenly, he was coming up short.

He shrugged.

"Look at me," the lieutenant commanded.

Will checked to see if Yoda was ticked. He didn't seem to be.

"Everyone knows you know more than you're saying. I won't order you to tell me. But you need to consider very carefully if you are better serving Gabe with your silence than you would with your words. Honor and loyalty are about all we have here, so I understand the predicament you're in. If you need a sounding board, I'm here."

DQ went back to his paperwork, dismissing further conversation. Will got up and left.

Cruz was not so philosophical when, fifteen minutes later, he slammed Will up against the lockers.

"The word of the day is chit-chat, Clancy," Cruz hissed, right in Will's face. "Did Suzanne kill Max?"

"I don't know."

Cruz was at least four inches taller than Will and far more powerful. If he wanted to, he could snap Will like a twig. But not without Will putting up a fight.

"What *do* you know, Clancy?"

If he didn't make his move now, he was screwed.

"I know that you better back off, Hollywood."

About the time he spit out *Hollywood*, Nic came through the door.

"Let go of him, Cruz. You're being a jerk."

Cruz glared into Will's eyes. Will did his best to glare back. Nic just stood there in the doorway, waiting.

At last, Cruz let go, muttered something about talking later, and stalked away, pushing past Nic on his way.

"What was that about?"

"Nothing," Will replied, and followed Cruz out.

Grisham was not pleased. But he did say she could stay. Claire wasn't inclined, at this point, to tell him that staying was the best way to accomplish her initial goal. He'd already agreed, and she hated whiners. So she thanked him and shut up to await further orders.

"Where are we at this point?" he asked.

"Chris is in booking, I'm changing into my uniform and will head over there soon to get him out of jail."

"Chris?"

"Gabriel, sir." Busted.

"Uh-huh. And you'll head over there after a stop at the Waffle House?"

"Don't know if they have Waffle House here, sir." Grisham, like Chris, was from Florida, where there was a Waffle House on every corner, kitty-corner from the inevitable WhataBurger. "And, yes, sir, I've already made that stop."

It never failed to amaze Claire how observant Grisham was. Most people were completely oblivious. He knew everything about each one of his people, including where they went for pre-trial rituals.

"Colonel, how was Gabriel as a lawyer?"

He laughed.

"Brilliant. The man could gentle the pants right off a witness. He's profoundly intelligent, soft spoken, and has amazing manners."

Not exactly the Chris Gabriel she'd seen so far. Again, evidence that she wasn't seeing the *real* man.

"You should be careful, Claire."

Grisham didn't use her first name often. When he did, he was sort of off the record.

"His charm is very subtle."

"Sir?" She thought she knew where he was going. Didn't like it much.

"You're already calling him Chris."

"He's my client, sir." Geez Louise.

"Whatever you say, Claire. All right," he said, as if sitting up straight after relaxing, "you keep me informed, and don't hesitate to use Brumby here to run stuff down. If you need anything else, just call him or me."

Claire had the best assistant in the entire JAG office. Senior Airman, soon to be Staff Sergeant Brian Brumbelow—she called him Brumby—had been in that office for just over two years. He was unobtrusive—no one really knew him—and very underrated. He was smart and had a way of getting around rules like no one she'd ever seen. His best quality, though, aside from being cute and cuddly, was that he was almost always two steps ahead of her. Since she was almost always two steps ahead of everyone around her, that was saying something.

"And, Captain, knock 'em dead."

"Will do, sir. Thanks."

Chris had expected the whole booking thing to take a bit longer. The clock on the wall of the interrogation room—they'd taken his watch and ring—indicated only an hour and a half had passed since he'd arrived. He sat, still in his flight suit—no orange jumpsuit until he was transferred to the county lock up—and waited, wishing he'd just wake the hell up. Every minute that ticked off the clock raised the tension in the tiny room. Torture by protracted inactivity.

It was another fifty minutes before Detective Medina, who now didn't even resemble the oh-so-courteous officer from his apartment that night, entered. He was definitely in bad bulldog mode, all puffed up and sure of himself. It was such crap.

"It will go better for you, Sergeant, if you just tell us about killing your friend."

Chris looked at him, then back at his hands. This guy had learned his technique from *Law and Order* reruns.

"We have all the evidence we need to convict you, Sergeant. If you tell us what happened now, I'll make sure there's a deal."

What part of "I *am* a lawyer" had this guy not understood? Did he honestly think that Chris would stupidly convict himself, even if he had murdered Max?

"Chris..."

"Don't *Chris* me, Detective. I...want...my...lawyer!"

Chris didn't get the chance to see the detective revert to good bulldog before the door opened, and one of his flunkies told him he was needed in his office.

Claire did not take the proffered seat. Instead, she straightened her back and waited. The looks she'd gotten when she walked in, in uniform this time, hair pulled back in a French braid, briefcase in hand, was almost laughable. It was a cross between fear and fantasy. It wasn't the first time she'd used that effect.

"I need to see Detective Medina."

"He's not available at the moment."

"Go get him. Tell him if he so much as sneezes at my client, I'll have him censured."

The guy clearly didn't know what "censured" meant, but he was sufficiently motivated to pivot briskly and head into the bowels of the building. The other clerk smiled tersely and offered her a seat. She just blinked at him.

Medina appeared exactly two minutes later and ushered her back to his office.

He, too, offered her a seat. She shook her head.

"I won't be here that long. I want to see my client."

"Tell me, *Lieutenant*, was the sergeant your client when you first got here? In which case you are a liar?'

Claire decided that the adversarial relationship needed to be dialed back a bit. She ignored his rank mistake and softened her stance.

"Look, Jim, we aren't enemies." Now *that* was a lie. "I told you the truth when I got here. I was here only to gather the facts. However, the closest JAG attorney, other than me of course, is at Travis Air Force Base. It was only logical that I take the case since I was standing right there."

"Some coincidence that was, Captain." His switch from lieutenant to captain was not lost on her.

"Not entirely, but I assure you I didn't know anything about a pending arrest. I was sort of the lucky winner of this case. So, here we are."

Medina eyed her with suspicion for another moment before backing off, for whatever reason.

"Fine, then."

"I need to see my client. Would you mind taking me to him?"

"Fine."

He still wasn't playing nicely.

He turned, and she followed him down the hall to an interrogation room. He opened the door a few inches, then hesitated with his hand on the knob.

"You didn't interrogate a man who had a lawyer, did you, Jim?"

Score one for the girl.

Jim clenched his teeth slightly. He pushed the door open and turned toward her.

She pounced, leaning in until she was mere inches from his face. The effect was satisfying.

"Naughty detective. Now, please leave me alone with my client, and don't even think about listening from the other side of the glass or whatever you have here in Merced. Because if you do that, and I find out, it could get, well, icky."

She stepped aside so he could get past, then walked through the door and closed it behind her.

After unbuttoning her jacket, she took the seat opposite Chris Gabriel who, for the first time since they'd met, was giving her a look of appreciation and respect.

"How's it goin', Champ?"

At this, he finally broke down and smiled, which blindsided her so completely that she had to look away to collect her thoughts.

Finally, a familiar face. A feisty familiar face, at that. The woman had Medina hogtied in seconds. Chris wondered where, exactly, the captain picked up the ability to lean in and invade a person's space like that. Most people were as uncomfortable doing it as was their target.

And then, that husky voice and a flash in her dark eyes added punch to her words.

For the first time this morning, he thought things might have turned in his favor. And, suddenly, hers was the very best face he could have seen.

Chapter Eleven

Chris's smile didn't last long. When he looked again at her, he was closed down, broadcasting nothing whatsoever.

"You know, Chris, I'm on your side here," she said, hoping to ease back into his confidence. "I can defend you without your help, but it sure would be easier if I had it."

"What papers do you need me to write for you, councilor?"

She shook her head at his snipe. When he didn't retreat, she pushed on.

"Give me a break," she said, leaning on the table, staring him down. Then she straightened up, pushed back her chair a bit and crossed her legs. "I need you to come clean, Chris."

"Fine. Here's what I know. I was on a mission up near Reno and when I got home, found Max Delati, one of my oldest friends, dead in my apartment."

He wanted to play games. Fine.

"Okay, Chris, here's what I know."

She let the sentence hang and watched as he silently rubbed his vacant ring finger on this right hand. He'd done that in his apartment, when he still had the ring. He had nice hands, gentle but strong.

"The wound that killed Max was clearly not self-inflicted. Why they said so in the beginning is beyond me. You and Max go way back, and he got the girl you wanted. Said girl just might be the one who had been sleeping in your bed when Max was killed. If the cops had identified her perfume—she wears Shalimar, doesn't she?—I'd know for sure. How am I doing?"

Chris's eyes narrowed, but he never broke eye contact. He didn't speak.

"The gun that was found in his hand, and purportedly inflicted the fatal shot, was yours, Chris."

His friends—heck, everyone that knew him—said Chris was a lousy liar, that he never lied. When he finally looked down, Claire realized that he was right on the edge of his abilities to hide.

"You called Max the day before you found him. And someone called your cell from your home phone on Thursday night. You might be able to answer for all these circumstances, Chris. But if you say nothing, you're looking pretty guilty."

"I'm not guilty, though, Claire."

It was the first time he'd used her first name. It came out like a plea for help, and her stomach twisted in response. Surprising herself, she reached across the table and laid her hand on top of his.

"I know."

Time hung suspended, her hand on his, their eyes locked. The room felt like it had closed in, focusing on that instant. As if eternity were forged right then.

Chris knew she believed him. This wasn't an act, wasn't her lawyer persona. This was Claire, and she was letting him see into her soul, see her passion for the truth, her trust in him, her heart.

He could trust her. He'd never felt that before with a woman. It wasn't the rip-off-your-clothes passion or the laughter-and-roses-and-sweet-kisses, either. Though both those things bubbled quietly beneath the surface, the prevailing feeling was an abiding fondness and respect.

"I'm sorry, Claire. I can't tell you more."

Another woman would have yanked her hand away, would have flounced away mad, would have demanded or cursed or something. But she didn't.

She squeezed his hand, and smiled—an almost conspiratorial smile—then slowly withdrew her hand and stood.

The woman looked great in uniform, by the way.

"Okay, I'll see if I can get you out of here. I assume you'll allow me to plead you not guilty?"

He merely nodded, suddenly aware that this quick and sudden attraction was completely insane. Post-traumatic stress—well, right-in-the-middle-of-traumatic-stress—disorder, big time.

When he saw next saw her, he was led into the courtroom along with three others who'd shared a holding cell with him for the past two hours. The clock they passed in the hall, on the way to the courtroom, said it was just before one.

The guard had brought in store-wrapped sandwiches and bottled water for lunch, presumably at noon. But Chris wasn't hungry, so he passed off his lunch to the hulking guy he'd taken to calling Bear—in his head, anyway.

Better to feed the beast his food than... He tried not to think about it.

He sat off in the corner, and though he tried not to, closed his eyes, suddenly more exhausted than he'd ever been. Days on the mountain in the snow didn't result in this kind of tired. Only massive amounts of tension did. That, and no sleep for days.

He was so tired, when the bailiff uttered the all-rise command, he had trouble getting to his feet.

Luckily, his case was called first, so he didn't have to sit and stand again. He made his way to the podium to stand beside the blazing beauty who was his attorney.

He was able to mumble "not guilty" when asked specifically by the judge how he pleaded and was able to nod and say "yes, sir" when asked if he understood this or that. Beyond that, he remembered little of what happened.

Once bail had been set at two hundred thousand dollars, the judge got very serious and yakked on and on, with Claire nodding and yes-sirring. It wasn't until the judge looked over across the room at a man standing in the back of the court room that Chris realized that Yoda was there, yes-sirring and nodding as well. Chris was swaying on his feet by the time Claire took his arm and whispered to him that she'd take care of everything.

Whatever everything was.

Claire called Eric just after one thirty.

"The bail's been set at two hundred thousand. If you go to a bail bondsman, you'll need to come up with collateral for the full amount. Ten percent you won't get back."

That was a lot to ask of a friend.

"Yeah, Captain, I'm aware of that. I've got it covered," he barked.

Prince Charming from—was it just yesterday?—was definitely gone, replaced with one stressed PJ. Either that, or this was his normal surliness, and the charm was a complete act. She started to speak when he continued.

"I'm sorry, Claire. I didn't mean to snap your head off."

Well, that answered that, she supposed.

"It's okay. Trying times."

"You got it. Have you eaten lunch yet?"

"Um, no. Late breakfast."

"Let me take you to lunch, then we'll go over and get the Angel out of hell. Are you at the hotel?"

"No, the courthouse."

"Give me fifteen minutes, and I'll be out front. Look for the bright yellow Wrangler—no top today. I'll look for the prettiest attorney in town."

Claire smiled. "I'm in uniform, flyboy."

"What do you know? So am I."

The line clicked dead without her even saying yes. Eric must be the man no one says no to.

Eric spotted her the moment he turned the corner. That was one hot officer. Thoughts of fraternization skittered through his head as he pulled up and reached over to open the door for her.

Gabe would have gotten out and walked around.

"Hey, Cap," he said as she gracefully maneuvered her tall body into the Jeep. "Where would you like to eat?"

"Mexican. Is there good Mexican food here, *Cruz?*"

He smiled at her playing with his name.

"Father is full-blooded Mexican, and Mom is Scandinavian. And, yes, there's a great little Mexican food place close by."

They rode in silence until they pulled into a parking place in front of Señor Manuel's. It was a hole-in-the-wall place that tourists missed. Tiny, with only a handful of tables. The hostess greeted them with a smile and ushered them to a table.

"*Cervesa* for either of you?" she asked.

Cruz waved her off. "Working. Sorry. Maybe next time."

"Iced tea with lemon, please," Claire said.

"Dew," Cruz followed.

She handed them the menus and told them their server would be with them in a moment. Cruz returned her smile.

"Do they always do that?" Claire asked, smirking.

"What?"

"Treat you like a god and anyone who's with you as simply an adjunct."

"I don't know what you mean."

"Yes, you do. Do they?"

"Yeah, pretty much."

She instantly liked this guy. It was one of those peas-in-a-pod things—she suspected that, if they filled out a survey, they'd answer the same on a lot of things. He was a little bit cocky and arrogant, in a good way, if there were such a thing, and immensely charming. Yet, there was an underlying trustworthiness and stability, a certain vulnerability.

Claire opened her menu. "What's good here?"

"Everything. My favorite is their chicken enchiladas."

"Works for me. Order away."

That done, he turned to Claire.

"So tell me about Captain Janova."

"Captain Janova would rather hear how a Sergeant in a rescue squadron can afford to bail his friend out of jail at that price."

Well, the girl was certainly direct. Not a girl, a woman for sure, yet there was something quite girlish about her.

"Ladies first."

"Fine," Claire said, taking a sip of her tea, reluctantly surrendering the *Reader's Digest* version of her life story—short and sweet. The longer version was hardly used. It was the one she brought out in the getting-to-know-you phase of a real relationship. That hadn't happened in years.

"I grew up in Colorado Springs. My dad left us when I was two. My mom is amazing. She's a Colorado state senator."

"Impressive."

"Yeah, she is. I became a lawyer and less than a year later, joined the Air Force."

"Wow, that's the wrong order."

"Tell me about it."

"What made you join?"

"Nine-Eleven."

Cruz just smiled and nodded. She couldn't remember ever telling anyone that and having them not nod. It was universally understood in a sad, tragic way. Even now.

"How long have you known Chris?"

"Only hours longer than I've known you. But you already knew that, didn't you?"

She was pretty sure that most of these questions were merely a formality. Eric Cruz was, somehow, a few steps ahead her. *Note to self: have Brumby check this guy out. As a matter of fact, have him check all these guys out.* Maybe she could keep this awkward situation—Cruz knowing far more about her than she knew about him—from happening again.

Eric neither acknowledged nor denied her accusation. He simply watched the waitress walk by as if he were interested.

"Your turn. You didn't seem phased when I told you the amount of the bail. Nor did you balk at flushing twenty thousand dollars just to get Chris out on bond. How does that work?"

"Investments."

She laughed. Now he was uncomfortable.

"Do you always hide who you really are or do you actually have something to hide, Sergeant?"

The waitress interrupted with the food, but Claire had a hunch Cruz could keep track of where they'd left off. Whether he *would* was the real question.

They ate in silence, only interjecting small talk along the way. But when he was done—long before she was—he pushed back his plate and eyed her closely.

"My father is the plastic surgeon to the stars. Money isn't really an object for me. Besides, Gabe is good for it."

She finished her bite and tried to come up with a good answer to that.

Before she could, he continued. "Did you know that the autopsy report came back this morning?"

She nearly choked. He was not just a *couple* steps ahead.

"Don't ask," he said to her next unspoken question. "But I have a copy in the car for you."

"And?"

"And the reason that there was so much blood on Gabe's rug is because the bullet pierced the descending aorta and he bled out in seconds." Cruz frowned.

There was more. "And?"

"And, since the wound was pretty much point blank, the coroner could not determine the height of the killer. Neither pointing to or away from Gabe."

"Damn."

"I'm no expert, but all the evidence I saw was circumstantial."

"I won't ask."

He winked. He actually winked. And she blushed.

"Who do you think was in his bed, Claire?" Cruz asked.

"He doesn't have a blonde girlfriend, by chance?"

"Angel?" Cruz laughed. "Hardly. The boy lives on a higher plane. He sometimes steps down from there to dally, but nothing even remotely permanent. He doesn't do one-on-one very well. Put him in a crowd, and he's a dazzler. But no, no blonde girlfriend, other than one from his distant past."

"Suzanne."

"Yeah, was it her?" Cruz asked.

"If it was, he's not saying," Claire said.

"He wouldn't."

"Not even to save his own life?"

"Not if he gave his word," Cruz answered, dead serious.

The conversation drifted into silence and Claire pushed away her own plate.

Once back to the car, Eric pulled a manila envelope from behind her seat. On it was written, in very neat block letters—all caps—CLARE

"If you get the DNA results before I do?" she asked.

"Of course. Okay with you if we stop at the bondsman's office on the way back to your car?"

It took thirty minutes for Cruz to sign away both his plane—it was only valued at just over one hundred eighty thousand dollars—and his brand new Jeep. His hand didn't even shake as he signed the papers, but his teeth were clenched. He wanted her to think he did this lightly.

That wasn't the case.

Cruz dropped her at the courthouse and met her again at the jail. They waited about half an hour for Chris to come out. When he did, Cruz flew to his side, steadying him. Chris looked even worse than he had this morning. Now, even his color looked wan.

At three thirty, they dragged him to her car. Cruz had tried to take him in his car, but Claire insisted. It was her ass on the line—hers and Lieutenant Quillen's, actually—if this guy disappeared. Even if he was in no condition to run, she wasn't letting him out of her sight until they came to a certain understanding. Eric refrained from reminding her that he had a great deal at stake as well.

In reality, though, it wasn't like Cruz was worried about his money. He was clearly worried about his friend. He followed her to Chris's apartment and practically carried him upstairs. At one point, Claire thought it would have been easier had Cruz thrown Chris over his shoulder and done just that. She gave them the courtesy of not intruding as Cruz got his friend into bed, something that Chris didn't even protest.

"I'll stay with him if you want," Eric said upon returning to the living room.

"I'll stay."

"Okay. Do you need anything?"

Eric had the door half closed behind him when she caught him.

"Actually, would you mind going by my room and getting my laptop?"

"I can do that."

"No snooping while you're there, Cruz."

"In your undies or your laptop?" he said with a grin, then reconsidered as the level of his insubordination occurred to him.

"Neither, Sergeant," she said, flashing him a smile, letting him off the hook.

"Yes, ma'am."

Chapter Twelve

One phone call got the ball rolling on a number of questions she had. Brumby was working on backgrounds for all the PJs on Bravo Squad, on Suzanne's recent medical problems, and on the finer points of California law.

That left her to read through the thirteen-page autopsy report—which she did after changing into the sweats that Eric had thoughtfully brought from her room. The fleece held on slightly to his obscenely expensive cologne. *Armani*, she thought.

The upshot of the autopsy: Max Delati was most definitely murdered. No surprise there, except to whatever genius had originally called it suicide.

That done, she began getting to know her client by wandering through his house. It would be crossing some ethical line to open doors and drawers, so she just took in what was visible. She didn't learn much.

He was neat and tidy, not given to clutter of any kind. He apparently liked movies or sports or something because he actually had a viewing room. Big screen TV and all the trimmings with two matching easy chairs set exactly in the right spot for watching.

The kitchen was spotless. Even the copper bottoms of the pots that hung there looked almost, but not quite brand new. The ice in the ice maker dropped as she walked around the kitchen, nearly making her jump out of her skin. She smiled at the silliness of that.

The bookshelves held an incredibly eclectic group of subjects. Emergency medicine and law, naturally. But there was also history, politics, and a smattering of science—physics, mostly—and math. The man had the full set of Blackstone's Commentaries on the Laws of England and a shelf of equally great books on common law. Claire fought the urge to pull them from the shelf. She couldn't fight the urge to drool.

At last, she ended up in the back of the apartment, where her client slept, oblivious to her presence.

A warrior had to be sick or past tired to do that or had to implicitly trust the person with him. That thought, oddly, made warmth spread through her. Cancel that warmth. He probably didn't even know she was there.

How long had she stood in the doorway watching him sleep?

Long enough to feel something she hadn't felt in a very long time. Or maybe ever.

"Where you been?" Will asked when Cruz arrived back at the Section—before remembering that he wasn't on Cruz's best-loved list at the moment. Then he cringed, waiting for the eruption that never came.

"Having lunch with Captain Janova, and then bailing Gabe out of jail."

"He's out?" Will jumped to his feet.

"On bail, Clancy. Only on bail."

"Where is he?"

"Home sleeping, with the good captain babysitting."

"Oh."

"Need to talk to him, do you?"

Damn.

"Not particularly. I'm just glad he's out."

"Yeah, right."

The spiraling conversation was interrupted when the lieutenant whistled from the hallway.

"Listen up everyone. New memo on the board. Colonel and Mrs. McIntyre will be in town this weekend for his farewell party. Party is Saturday night. Who has the gift?"

"I do," Nic's voice from another part of the building. "I'll dust it off."

The gift, a large framed print of Mac's Black Hawk refueling in mid-air with everyone's signatures on the mat, had been with Nic since the first Hail and Farewell had been canceled because of a mission. They'd hailed the incoming colonel—Colonel Scott—a week later. But, by then, Mac and Lily had left for the Academy.

The lack of enthusiasm evident in Nic's voice spoke for all of them, Will thought. What, under different circumstances, would have been a fun party, now had a black cloud hanging over it.

Maybe something good would happen before then.

Like what?

Like the real murderer would prance into the police department and clear things up?

That is, if Gabe really didn't do it.

Icy cold fear shot down Will's spine, followed by a hollow feeling of betrayal in the pit of his stomach. Betrayal. Either one of his best friends had killed a rival for a woman—something Will couldn't quite picture Gabe doing—or *he'd* just betrayed that friend by even questioning his innocence. Either way, he was betraying someone with his silence.

"I'm leaving for the day," Will announced to no one in particular. Then, with heavy footsteps, he walked out of the Section.

Claire found peanut butter and jelly, along with some bread whose freshness was rather questionable. She settled for ice water to drink.

Her client hadn't moved. Once, she'd even gone back and watched to make sure he was still breathing.

Sandwich in hand, she dragged out the crime scene photos and wandered back to where Max's body had been found. The rug had been removed and, if she looked carefully, she could tell where the blood had seeped into the wood floor. How many hours had Chris worked to erase what, apparently, wasn't erasable?

What was Max was doing standing here? The crime scene photos indicated that he had a glass of wine in his hand. The other glass was untouched on the kitchen counter. Who was he waiting for? His wife? Chris? Someone else?

The pictures on the wall caught her eye, and she moved closer, almost stepping over a phantom body that was no longer there. Chris had prints of his family, all sisters, a few from their childhood. He had a framed postcard celebrating the fiftieth anniversary of the Air Force Academy. One frame held a variety of snapshots of his teammates. Missing was any hint of a career with JAG, nothing from law school, and no pictures of Max or Suzanne. Was it that easy for him to put away his past?

Her thoughts were interrupted by the ringing of a cell phone—not hers. She followed the sound to the front hall where Chris's things were still in a zipper bag with his name and social security number on it. The phone inside rang again.

She retrieved the phone. Caller ID showed a familiar number.

"Hello." Might as well not tip her hand yet.

"Who is this?"

As suspected, it was Suzanne.

"This is Claire Janova, Suzanne."

"Claire?" There was a long pause. "What are you..." Another long pause. "Is Chris okay?"

"Well, other than being arrested for murdering *your* husband, I guess he's fine. But he didn't murder Max, did he, Suzanne?"

Suzanne didn't answer, and after a few moments, she hung up.

Claire looked at the phone as if it could tell her where Suzanne was. Then she returned it to the bag, pausing only momentarily to examine the Air Force Academy ring in the bag. The ring Chris twisted when under stress. Putting it back, she went to find her own phone.

"Cruz."

"Eric, it's Claire."

"Chris okay?" he asked, his voice a little panicked.

"He's still asleep. He's still breathing, so I assume so."

"Okay..."

"Suzanne just called his cell phone. Since you're the magic man, can you trace her call?"

"Not after the fact."

"Damn. You know the cops won't put a trap on his line for us. They have their killer. We need her, Eric."

"Yeah, we do. She's not using her credit cards, or Max's for that matter."

"Do I want to know how you know that?" she asked.

"Magic, like you said," he answered, his voice laced with humor. "Let me see what I can do with his phone. I'll let you know."

"Good."

"Claire, he won't like us doing this."

"Tough. Thanks, Eric."

She put her phone back in her briefcase and sat down on the couch. The street below the front windows was quiet now that it was dark. Down the block, there was one place open. She couldn't tell what it was. But other than that, it was pretty dead—at least after the hourly *bonging* of the clock across the street. *That* was loud. Loud enough that she wondered how Chris slept through it.

The quiet crept up from below, settling somewhere inside her. She closed her eyes for a moment. An hour later, still way too early to really go to bed, she settled for just lying down on the couch.

"Cruz."

"Hey, Hotshot."

It was the voice he most wanted and least wanted to hear. Months had passed since he'd run from Kit Sheridan's place to escape a fire burning nearly out of control. For days, he had screened all his calls, afraid she was pissed and would call to scream at him for leaving her like that. Even more, he was afraid she wouldn't call.

She didn't.

He'd run into her a time or two since. Each time, it had been like that evening had never happened. She was the same old Kit that drove him crazy, one minute smiling, and the next calling him names.

It was only recently he'd begun to dread a phone call from her again—this time because he was up to no good and definitely didn't want to be caught. The chances of her finding out beforehand, though, were slim to none. Afterward was another matter altogether. He was reasonably safe at this point.

"Hi, Kit."

"Want to take me out for a drink?"

"Why?"

"No reason. C'mon. Meet me at McGill's. Half an hour?"

McGill's had, over the last few months, become her bar—the Oasis, his. Though, on occasion, the lines crossed, it seemed like they'd come to a silent understanding somehow. Or maybe he was just loony tunes. Or maybe both.

"Okay."

Driving over there, he kicked himself. If he'd wanted a drink—and the stress level right now might warrant one or twelve—he could either go to the refrigerator or call one of the guys. But this chick had an uncanny way of getting him to say yes to all the wrong things.

"Hollywood," he said as he turned the corner before the bar, "you will not have sex with that woman."

She was waiting at a back table with a pitcher and two frosty glasses. He walked toward her while she poured.

"Hey," she said.

"Hey, yourself." God, he was rendered woefully inadequate by this girl. That was unacceptable.

"You hear that Mac's coming back this weekend?"

"Yeah, I did."

Kit had kept up on Mac's recovery, his retirement, and his move. She always said she had an interest since he was one of her success stories. Not just any helicopter pilot could fly into those conditions and pluck a victim from the side of a mountain, she said. True enough, but Cruz wasn't inclined to feed her ego by agreeing.

"How's business?"

"Good."

The way it rolled off her tongue, with no hesitation whatsoever made him wonder if she really believed that. He smiled to himself.

"I need an invite to that party, Cruz. I didn't get a chance to say goodbye to the colonel."

"Ahh. So, you invited me here under false pretenses?"

"Well, of course. Why else would I invite you to buy me a drink—you're paying, by the way."

"Fine."

"Fine to paying, or fine to taking me to the party?"

"Whatever, Kit." Cruz suddenly felt tired. He let his chin drop to his hand and let out his breath.

"I heard about Gabriel."

Figured.

"You decided to let me take you out for drinks so you could get all the good gossip on Angel?"

She waited to answer until he looked up.

"Listen, Hotshot, I'm not much into gossip. Who would I talk to, anyway? I just thought you might... Oh, never mind."

She got up to leave, and he caught her elbow.

"I'm sorry. Please stay."

She looked down at his hand on her arm, then up at him, her green eyes flashing an excuse-me look. Then they warmed, and she tossed her head.

"C'mon, flyboy, let's dance."

Another big mistake. Holding her close, moving to the mellow music, felt way too good. Kissing her felt even better. Her lips were warm, wet, and welcoming.

Abruptly, though, she stepped back and raised an eyebrow.

"My turn to say no, Hotshot."

He followed her back to the table where she finished her beer. Then after kissing him on the cheek and telling him to hang in there, she left.

He killed the pitcher by himself.

Claire was awakened by sunshine in her eyes, then startled by the silhouetted figure that stood stock still in the doorway to the living room. She jumped up, prepared to do battle with the phantom, then realized that it was Chris. He stood, staring at her, wearing only his boxer shorts. She turned away.

"How long have you been awake?" she asked.

"About two minutes longer than you, I guess. What are you doing on my couch?"

She looked up at him, trying not to notice how amazing he was. "I would think that was fairly obvious."

"Okay, counselor, let me rephrase. Why are you sleeping on my couch?"

She stepped in close. "To make sure you don't jump bail and leave me hanging."

He didn't back up. People usually backed up when you got into their space. He just looked her up and down, and then stepped around her on his way to the kitchen. There, he opened the fridge and pulled out a Pepsi, holding it up to offer her one.

"No, thanks."

When he returned, he hesitated beside her until she glanced up at him. His hair was slightly rumpled, but other than that, he looked much better than he had since she'd met him. His tan skin looked, well, tan. His grey eyes were sharp and clear.

"And you could have stopped me if I'd fled?"

Ordinarily, a line like that from a guy would have been accompanied by at least a slight leer. From Chris—nothing.

"Nope. But I can have your bail revoked."

"And you think I'd do that to Eric?"

While she watched, he tipped the can to his lips and drank, his eyes never leaving hers.

"No."

"Then why are you here?"

"Because I think you might do it to me."

He smiled ruefully.

"I give you my word. I won't leave. Now, will you please go away, and give me a bit of privacy?"

She was first to break eye contact—and it ticked her off.

"Fine. I'll be back later. We have some things to talk about." She looked at her watch for the first time. It was already eight thirty. When was the last time she'd slept past five? She needed to leave, swim, have coffee, and get some perspective.

Most of all, she just needed to leave.

He watched as she gathered her laptop and briefcase. She was nearly to the door when she stopped.

"By the way, Suzanne called while you were asleep."

She dropped the bomb and pulled the door open, sliding it closed on a very quiet champion. Score one for the girl who had to look away first.

There was nothing for Chris to do about it, but go take a shower. He had no control over anything anymore, it seemed. And now Claire knew that Suzanne was in the picture, even if she hadn't known before. Maybe it was the time to get Cruz involved, to tell all of them everything. Maybe Yoda was right, and he needed to let people help him.

He turned on the water and let it hit his chest for a time, lost in thought.

He wasn't opposed to help. That was just stupid pride. He'd given Suzanne his word that he wouldn't tell that she was there. But he hadn't exactly kept it, and his phone call had brought Max here.

To die.

And while he didn't believe she'd murdered Max, she might very well have killed him. In self-defense.

Not very likely since the shot was point blank.

Bending to let the water run over his bowed head, he tried to imagine what had happened here.

He needed more information. What had come between Max and Suzanne to the point that she seemed afraid of him?

Suddenly, a light went on somewhere in his brain, and he cursed himself for not seeing sooner. Suzanne had exhibited classic bi-polar behavior—one minute paranoid, next angry, then manic. Classic. He was trained to see stuff like that.

He needed to find out if she was being treated.

What was he saying? Just because you're paranoid doesn't mean someone's not out to get you.

He turned off the water and grabbed his towel.

How did he get more information without betraying Suz's confidence? It was possible she was a victim in all this and that she was still in danger.

It was even more possible that he was a complete moron.

Chapter Thirteen

Claire had been swimming laps since high school swim team and could estimate, by the size of almost any pool, how many lengths equaled a meter. Today, her usual fifteen hundred to two thousand meters only slightly took the edge off the tension that held her taut.

It would have been acceptable—though not entirely so—if it were the case that had her tied up. But it wasn't. And she hated that.

The feelings that had her swimming harder today could ruin her career. But worse than that—if there was a worse than that—was what that could mean for her client. It could mean that she wasn't on top of her game. And that could do far more than end his career.

At roughly one thousand meters, she stopped, tugged off her goggles, and downed the bottle of water that sat at the far end of the pool.

She simply had to get a grip.

By ten, she was out the door with her second Styrofoam cup of coffee in her hand. She made a mental note to look in the car for her travel mug. By ten seventeen, she was walking in the Jolly Green Giant steps toward the Section.

This was the first time she'd arrived in uniform and the PJs' response was markedly different. The last time, they'd been guys. This time they were airmen, standing at attention as she passed by on her way to the lieutenant's office.

Quillen, too, quickly stood at attention when she entered his office unannounced, his clerk elsewhere at the moment.

She shut the door behind her.

Will had watched her walk into the building. The woman wore an Air Force uniform very well. Her hair was pulled up, and she walked with a determination that only made her gender more obvious. She oozed both professionalism and beauty. It was a striking contrast. Polished.

Cruz merely smiled when Will entered the locker room.

"She's in with Yoda. Door closed."

"Lucky Yoda," Will muttered then realized how that came out. Too late to take it back, Cruz chuckled.

"Did you see Captain JAG," Cowboy whispered, sneaking into the locker room as if he wasn't supposed to be there.

"Kinda hard to miss," Cruz replied.

"Woo-wee, she's one fine lookin' lawyer."

Sometimes the conversations of his team mates drove Will crazy. This was one of them. He shook his head and left the room.

Fifteen minutes later, he watched the captain walk by the dayroom, followed closely by Cruz. Will wandered out far enough to watch the two of them talk before the lady continued to her car and drove off.

Cruz hadn't found a way to tap into Chris's phone—at least not one that wouldn't get him arrested. Maybe that was better. But her mojo was back, at least for the moment because she'd managed to convince the lieutenant not to restrict Chris to the barracks, which by all rights, he could have done. She had to hope her mojo held, because she was off to see Colonel Tom Scott, Chris's commander. It was, ultimately, his call.

She found the colonel at the airfield, having just landed. He was about the same height as Chris—but bulkier. He reminded her of Magnum P.I. His mustache wasn't quite as cheesy. He had such a deep Southern accent that, once he spoke, the similarity faded.

"Captain, you're the one representing Gabriel?"

"Yes, sir."

He stopped his long strides and turned to face her.

"What can I do for you?"

"Ground Gabriel, but please don't restrict him to the barracks."

One eyebrow raised slightly on his handsome face.

"And why would I do that, Captain?"

"Because he's innocent."

When that didn't seem to move him to agree, she continued. "Because if he's there, in his apartment, we'll have a better chance of catching the real murderer, sir."

"How's that?"

"I'm afraid I can't tell you that, sir, but I assure you there are good reasons for him to be there." Complete bluff. If he called her on it, she was screwed. "I will take complete responsibility for his being there."

"It doesn't work that way, and you know it, Captain. But, for now, I'll do as you ask."

"Thank you, sir."

"Anything else?"

"No, sir."

"Then have a nice day, Captain."

Two for two, regardless of the reasoning. She'd take what she could get.

Her phone rang as soon as she left the base.

"Captain Janova."

"Captain, this is Debbie Brooks, clerk of the court for Merced County. I have your client scheduled for preliminary hearing on Monday at ten in the morning."

"Wow, that soon?"

"Yes, we had an opening, and the district attorney requested the slot. Do you have any objection?"

"No, Ms. Brooks, that will be fine. Thank you for calling."

Claire pocketed her phone and gritted her teeth.

Two out of three.

Damn it all.

The next call evened the score, though it suddenly felt like she was behind—way behind. It was Cruz. The blonde hair in Chris's bed was a positive match for Suzanne Johannsen.

Yoda had informed Chris by phone that he was not going to be required to move onto base. He was clear it had taken Captain Janova pulling out all the stops to make that happen. However, Chris would be on restricted duty. He'd be grounded from missions and would work on the PJ-do list that had become quite long. He'd report back at 0800 tomorrow.

Oh, joy.

After the call, Chris paced around his apartment until he'd driven himself right up the wall. He threw on his old jeans and went next door to lay the wood floor in the living room.

He opened all the windows and turned on the fan, but that didn't seem to help much. He'd only worked for about an hour, pounding the tongue and groove panels into place with a rubber mallet. Sweat poured down his chest, and he felt wrung out.

He pushed up from the floor and went to the windows to enjoy the breeze. The traffic below was steady and people walked up and down the street, stopping here and there to look into the shop windows.

A sudden hopelessness swept over him. If the truth didn't triumph here, he might not look out on this street for long. In his years studying law, then practicing law, he'd never considered being on this side of the system. Of having his future in the hands of total strangers.

His life had, many times, been in the hands of his team mates, sometimes in the hands of people he hadn't met on a rescue team. But there was an unspoken trust there. A person wasn't likely to even get on a sophisticated rescue team without proving their ability. God help everyone if they did. He knew that was true for the PJs—hell, only one in ten even made it onto the teams. And Daniel Fraser, the top gun of the civilian SAR unit in Yosemite—a former SEAL—was almost fanatical about standards and keeping his team in shipshape, no pun intended.

Yet, here he was, facing a future where the definition of wide-open spaces became an exercise yard of less than an acre.

He'd been helpless to stop his best friend from putting his money on the line for him, even though every time he thought about it, his stomach lurched. Yes, he was grateful to be out on bond, but it grated on him that he'd been at Cruz's mercy. Since then, he'd racked his tired brain for a way to redeem the situation on his own terms. In the meantime, he couldn't quite bring himself to talk to Cruz, even though he knew how that looked to everyone.

Probably even to Claire.

"God," he said through clenched teeth and slid down to the floor.

Claire stopped at the motel and changed into jeans, then headed over to re-re-interview her obstinate client.

The street door was propped open, so she went right up. Before getting to his door, though, she noticed that the apartment across the hall stood open. A fan blew the fresh air that drifted up from the street into what she could see was an apartment under remodel.

She walked in.

And there was Chris, sitting on the floor against the front wall, just under the windows, wearing only raggedy jeans—holes in both knees—with his head propped on his folded arms.

"Hey, Champ."

He looked up, his expression sober, then pushed to his feet.

"Hi."

Okay, he looked way too good this morning wearing only boxers. But in jeans, no shirt—it was distracting to say the least.

"Put some clothes on. We have to talk."

"Yes, ma'am," he said with just the slightest rebellion in his soft voice.

Five minutes later, he'd thrown on a t-shirt and offered her a soda.

"I don't suppose you have iced tea?"

"Nope, sorry."

"Then ice water, I guess."

She eased onto a barstool on the opposite side of the kitchen counter.

"What's up?" he asked as he sat and slid a glass across to her. He took a long drink from the Pepsi in his hand.

"We have a prelim set for Monday afternoon."

"Good."

"Good? Don't you think that's a little quick, Chris? That just doesn't happen."

"It does in a small town, I guess."

"It doesn't give us much time to prepare."

"Yeah, well, between the two of us, we can put it together by then. Their case is strictly circumstantial."

Chris was not naive enough to believe that circumstantial evidence didn't get people convicted all the time.

"And just how are we supposed to answer when the D.A. asks how it was that the victim's wife was sleeping in your bed?"

He shrugged, something she'd noticed he did when he was unwilling to answer.

Before she could stop, the question was out of her mouth. "Were you sleeping with Suzanne?"

He hardly reacted, except to turn an icy stare her way. Maybe the pulse in his neck picked up. He was silent for a moment, then spoke. "Do you believe I killed Max?"

"No, Chris, but..."

"Then do your job, Claire. Come up with other possibilities."

"And maybe you could stop being such a jerk." She slid off the stool, picked up her things and left. Without looking back.

Claire put the task of coming up with plausible defenses on the back burner. Over the years, she'd found that, if she tasked her brain with a job, then thought about other things, she'd usually have the answers when she needed them.

Some answers she needed sooner rather than later. These answers were beginning to feel personal. What was Suzanne Johannsen doing in Chris's bed, if not the obvious?

Chris had neither acknowledged nor denied sleeping with Suzanne. Backing up a step, he'd actually never admitted that she was even there. Only the evidence proved that.

For this afternoon, she'd work on putting together all she needed for the preliminary hearing. Some of the paperwork, she could task to Brumby. Some of it she preferred to do herself.

Chris's progress on the floor stopped when he realized that he'd put two rows down in the exact same order, with the breaks in the wood lining up. The last row would have to be redone. He couldn't remember ever feeling so distracted, so unable to concentrate. Even when he decided to nap, he couldn't get his mind quiet enough to sleep. Before this, he had no idea that a woman's perfume hung onto a room even after all the bedding was washed—twice. Either that, or the scent was just more evidence that he was losing it.

He lay on his back, staring at the ceiling. His mind drifted as he tried to come up with his own defense. Other than the truth, which was stranger than fiction, he had nothing.

Then his mind settled on Claire, her hair, her eyes, her body. More than that, though. He was drawn to her because, in the face of overwhelming odds, she believed him.

Cruz took a seat in the LT's office.

"So, where are we?" DQ asked.

"I don't know, sir. The DNA is back and shows irrefutably that Suzanne was in Gabe's bed. You know, even before the body was found, he acted strangely. He didn't start lying *after* Max was dead. He started *before*."

"Your thoughts?" the LT asked.

"I don't know what to think," Cruz admitted. "David?"

DQ glanced up at the use of his first name. But words were stuck.

"Tell me what you're thinking."

It took a while for Eric to answer. He didn't want to tell anyone what he was thinking. He didn't even want to admit those thoughts to himself.

"Eric."

And Yoda, the all-wise one, knew it.

"Loving a woman can make you do things...cripes." He scrubbed his fingers through his hair, then over his mouth and wished fervently that he hadn't voiced that thought.

Once it was out there, it was all too real.

Yoda sighed and drummed his fingers on the desk briefly before looking up at Cruz.

"He needs us to believe in him."

Cruz stood, hoping he was dismissed. "Yes, sir."

DQ frowned, then stood as well. "You can go, Cruz. But keep digging."

Cruz turned to leave.

"You might want to give him a call, Eric."

"He won't take my calls, sir."

Claire paced, finding it hard to refrain from thinking about Chris and Suzanne. She'd been on the phone twice with Brumby, and each time, he filled her in on the office gossip.

Apparently, the odds in the office pool were running five to one—no, make that six to one—that Chris Gabriel had been carrying on an affair for years with Suzanne and finally offed Max so they could be together. Well, the carrying on an affair part was the brainchild of Airman Landon in the mail room and was fast becoming a part of the story. Suzanne had never been a favorite with the women in the office, more because she had snagged Max, who remained an icon of male prowess—and a playboy—than because Suzanne, herself was a player.

"Do you believe all that crap, Brian?"

"No, I'm just the reporter, ma'am."

"What do *you* think?"

"I think that Max and Suzanne were both players, but they still seemed to be together, you know?"

"I wasn't there long enough to form an opinion."

"Yeah, right. Like you're ever at a loss for an opinion."

She laughed. He was right. The fact was, though, in this case, she hadn't cared enough to pay any attention.

"What other possibilities are there?" Claire asked.

"Well, the police on this end never suspected anything untoward going on. They searched the house thoroughly when Max reported Suzanne missing. They didn't find anything, to my knowledge. If Max was ever a suspect in her disappearance, they cleared him quickly enough."

"You know, Brian, we need those police reports, as well. Maybe we're missing something."

"Odds are, ma'am, that the office has it right."

"Screw the odds, Brumbelow. Chris Gabriel did not kill Max."

That maybe came out a bit more shrewish than she intended.

"Yes, ma'am."

"Get those reports and email them to me."

"Will do. And Claire?"

"Yeah."

"If you say he's innocent, then I'm with you all the way."

"Thanks. Later."

Despite the bit of fall in the air, she slipped into her suit, grabbed her goggles and a towel, pulled her hair into a ponytail, and headed for the pool. She needed to get her focus back.

Eric's eyes were beginning to glaze over as he stared at the screen of his laptop. He'd spent the last hour and a half paging through Suzanne's credit card charges covering the past year. He wanted to call Chris.

The woman could spend some money. But there was nothing significant. Up until two months ago, she spent nearly a thousand dollars a month on girl stuff—clothes, shoes, massages, make-up. She'd fit right in on Rodeo Drive. Scratch that. On Rodeo Drive, you could drop a grand on a t-shirt.

Two months ago, the spending stopped as if someone shut off the tap. Either something had dramatically changed in her life, or she'd simply switched to another card that Cruz hadn't found yet. Maybe Gabe knew.

He picked up the phone, then put it down again.

Gabe.

If the guy would even admit to having an affair with Max's wife. But that was so completely out of character for Angel. Okay, so, at least he could admit and explain her presence there—in his bed.

When had he stopping trusting Angel? Angel was, next to Nic, Eric's best friend in the world. When had this thing come between them?

He picked up the phone again and dialed.

"I'm not available. Leave a message." So like Chris—crisp and to the point—whereas Cruz changed his message weekly with another silly one. Right now, it said "Hi. I'm probably home, I'm just avoiding someone I don't like. Leave me a message, and if I don't call back, you'll know it's you."

No matter.

"Hey, man. Call me." If Gabe wanted crisp and to the point, he could do that.

Back to the computer screen. Maybe it was time to dig into Max a bit more. Another hour passed, and Eric's eyes began to cross with boredom.

Max spent money in much the same way his wife did. He got regular massages, spent money at Nordstrom, and apparently, loved good Italian food. Or, at least, expensive Italian food. Unless he was feeding his whole neighborhood.

Cruz wondered about the regular payment of twelve hundred dollars to *NWF Property Management*. Most people didn't put their rent on a charge card, but who knew? He made a mental note, then thought that perhaps Claire knew.

When she didn't answer—another no nonsense voicemail message, maybe Gabe had found his perfect match—he left a message.

He'd barely hung up when his phone rang. By the time he hung up again, he had a Thursday evening appointment with the owner of the delinquent note on Kit Sheridan's plane. That meeting was well worth missing poker for.

He closed the laptop and headed for the O.

Chapter Fourteen

The harder Chris tried to ignore the stirrings inside, the more he wanted to see Claire. He'd heard about clients fixating on their defense attorney, thinking that there was more to the relationship. He'd even had it happen once. But he was seriously not the type to let that kind of thing happen. Though, admittedly, he'd never been on this end of things, needing someone to save him.

Aside from the terrible feeling of having to rely on another person to do their job so that he could keep his life—actually, he did that all the time, but in an entirely different context—he hated the thought that he'd let himself fall for his attorney. That just couldn't happen.

For the next half hour, he made notes on a yellow pad from his desk drawer—old habits and whatnot—of all the things she needed to be doing to get him acquitted. The ones that implicated Suzanne in any way, he left off the list. Then, he pushed to his feet and grabbed his car keys.

Now, standing beside his car, he reconsidered. Maybe it was the moment he saw her gliding through the water, heedless of the fact that he watched. She wore a one piece suit, black, sleek, very like her. The way she moved through the water was fascinating, and not just a little bit fabulous.

He wandered over to the nearest trash can and deposited the yellow pad. If she trusted him, he was going to have to trust her.

Suddenly, a rib-eye from his favorite steakhouse in Le Grand sounded like a really good idea. Taking Claire there sounded even better.

He found a nearby pool chair and sat down, very much enjoying the sight, even more enjoying her single focus—speeding to the end of the pool, flipping around expertly, and repeating the process. If she knew he was there, she wasn't letting that deter her.

At five hundred meters, Claire stopped long enough to knock back the bottle of water she'd brought. At a thousand, she pulled herself from the water and slicked the water from her face. Then, she walked to where she left her towel, reached for it, and was headed back to her room when his voice stopped her.

"I'm not sure oblivious is a good trait in a lawyer."

She turned to see him sitting—more like lounging—his long legs stretched out before him—at the far end of the pool.

"I'm not sure stalking is a good trait in a client."

He just laughed.

It sounded really nice.

He'd changed out of the ratty jeans and cut up t-shirt—more's the pity—and was wearing cargo shorts and a Hawaiian shirt.

"What's up?" she asked.

"Even oblivious attorneys need to eat."

"True. Do you have a plan?"

"I do. Go get dressed."

"I didn't bring my matching muumuu, I'm afraid."

"Are you dissing my favorite shirt?"

"If that's your favorite shirt...well, I'm just not sure what that says about you, Sergeant."

"Go get dressed, ma'am. Dinner's on me."

"You might regret that, Sergeant."

The concern that crossed his face—probably because he'd just told an officer to go get dressed—was quickly replaced when he realized she wasn't taking him to task.

"Really, why?"

"'Cause I'm a big eater." She smiled at him and turned toward her room, almost wishing that he'd follow her. This time, she didn't even scold herself for the thought. This time, she actually allowed herself to wish.

Claire returned to where he sat at the pool in a matter of minutes, which was probably a good thing. He was having a tough time keeping his butt in the chair. If he'd followed her, then he would most certainly be making love to her right now.

Sure, he wanted that, almost to distraction, but there was depth to this woman that made him want to jump in, and not come out until he knew all of her hidden places intimately. Not just sexually. She felt comfortable to him, like he didn't have to talk or be something he wasn't.

That was a hard place to find with a woman. With anyone, for that matter.

And yet, he couldn't even come clean with her. There were lies between them—his lies—and that crushed any possibility for something more.

Now, Highway 99 South was filled with rush-hour traffic. He pulled the 'Vette back into the right lane, letting a Suburban with a *Baby on Board* sticker in the back window pass.

"You'll be glad to know the office odds, back at JAG, are six to one against you."

"I'll be glad to know that?"

"Indeed. I'd have thought they'd be higher."

"That makes me feel better."

She smiled over at him, her eyes sharp with humor, her dimples accentuating how beautiful she really was.

"Where'd you grow up, Claire?"

"Colorado Springs."

"The Springs, huh? Military brat?"

"No."

"Dated many Zoomies?" Chris asked.

"Zoomies?"

"Guys at the academy."

"Not really, most of them were too full of themselves." Again, with the grin.

"So now you're holding the Academy against me?"

"Not at all."

"Good. Is your family still there?"

"My dad left when I was two. Died when I was twelve. I saw him twice. My mom is a state senator and still lives in the house I grew up in."

"Impressive."

"That's what Cruz said. You're both right. She is an amazing woman. She held down a full-time job and was a city councilman for most of my teen years. Yet, somehow, she always knew where I was and what I was doing."

"And what's the plan for the rest of your life, then? Politics, or a family?" He hadn't intended to go *there*. Too late.

"Neither, I think. I'm too much of a vagabond. Too many places to see, too much to do. If I'd known what I know now, I'd have let the Air Force teach me to fly. Then I'd bail for an airline, jumpseating my way around the world."

"You aren't happy in JAG?"

"No, it's fine. Just have to squeeze in my passions when I can."

She stopped and looked away, obviously knowing that the last statement had come off with an element she hadn't intended. Chris followed the Suburban off the highway onto the two-lane that led to the restaurant.

He let her off the hook.

"Where have you been?"

"Greece. Spain. My next priority is Paris."

"Damn!"

The Suburban had stayed about a hundred yards ahead of them. With no warning, an SUV came from a road off to the right and plowed into the Suburban, throwing it right into oncoming traffic.

"Call nine-one-one, Claire," Chris said as he slowed and pulled off the road. The Suburban was hit again, head on, this time by a Mercedes that didn't have time to swerve.

Claire called on her cell, explaining their location and the need for fire and ambulance as she watched Chris sprint toward the scene. She hung up, after giving the dispatcher her number, then stuffed the phone in her pocket and climbed out of the 'Vette.

It was deathly quiet.

"Jump kit, behind my seat," he hollered on the fly. "Grab it, please."

Even in emergency mode, he was courteous.

She grabbed the bag—red canvas with a black medical snake—and ran toward the cars, wishing she'd worn her Nikes instead of sandals.

Chris was at the first car with the driver-side door open. She handed him the bag.

A child in a car seat screamed. Dad, not belted in, had been thrown over on Mom, who was belted in. Her seat was tipped at an odd angle. She had a cut on her forehead that bled freely into her eyes. She was just now coming around.

"What can I do?"

"Did you call?"

"Yes."

"Then stand here, and talk to these people. Tell them not to move and reassure them that the baby seems to be okay." He backed out of the window and glanced at her. "I'll go check the others."

Even now, the sound of distant sirens.

Thank goodness.

It was only minutes before both fire and ambulance were on scene. They must not have been as far into God-knows-where as Claire had thought.

She stood back and watched.

The medics were doing their thing and Chris was not interfering. He was crouched down on the side of the road in front of the car seat he'd pulled from the back of the car, kid still in it. He'd assured the medics that the baby appeared to be fine and that he'd keep an eye on her while they loaded their other patients.

The baby had stopped crying as Chris talked to her. He'd grabbed a small teddy bear from his jump bag and played peek-a-boo with the little girl, eliciting smiles between her huge gulps of air—leftovers from her crying so hard. Claire didn't know which one tugged at her heart more—the sweet tiny girl whose parents were fighting for their lives or the tall, hunky man who soothed her.

Another ambulance arrived and took the child from him, but not before he'd given them a very thorough assessment of her condition and not before another tumbler in Claire's heart fell into place.

Chris chaffed at the traffic resulting from the crash. He was starving. The last ten miles of their trek took over an hour, leaving plenty of time to talk.

"Does that happen often?" Claire asked.

"What?"

"You getting to do your hero thing?"

He just shook his head. "Actually, when I first got out of paramedic school, I looked for stuff like that to happen. Ached for it to happen. My theory was, if something horrible was going to happen, then let me be there to play. Kinda morose, isn't it?"

She nodded, smiling, turned toward him.

"It hardly ever happens, though. Cruz and I delivered a baby at the mall a few months back, though. That was cool. I did all the work, and she named the baby after Cruz. Unbelievable."

"You did *all* the work?"

"Well, she did some of it, I guess."

He loved the way Claire smiled. Loved the way they could just talk.

"You were pretty impressive back there, Champ."

"Thank you. I didn't do anything. But, thank you."

"It's my turn. Where did you grow up, Chris?"

"Florida."

"Yeah? You don't strike me as a beach bum. Cruz, yes. You no."

"Would it help if I told you I was blonde until my mid-teens?"

"Yes, that would definitely help. What part of Florida?"

"East coast, Boynton Beach, about halfway between West Palm Beach and Boca Raton."

"Family?"

"Four sisters, all younger."

"Wooo, that must have been fun. Lucky them having a big brother like you."

He didn't know what to say to that.

She continued. "I always wanted a big brother."

He wasn't about to say anything to that.

"So, you went to the Academy, then to law school, then resigned your commission and went into the champion business?"

What the hell did that mean? One thing for sure, it was cold water in his face. Probably a good thing. He was getting too comfortable.

The restaurant came into view before he could formulate a retort. Another good thing. His reply might have been snide.

Claire saw his look when she'd let her mouth get away from her. That wouldn't happen again. Not only did it make her sound like a haughty bitch, it had also stung him. She was set to apologize when he pulled into the parking lot. By the time he made it around to open her door and reached out to help her get out, the moment was lost, along with the sweet intimacy that they'd had on the trip.

All through dinner—which was excellent, just as he'd said—she tried to grab it back, but everything she said just kinda sputtered and died as soon as it came out.

She'd say something inane, and he'd blow out his breath through his nose and put on a smile, something Claire was coming to recognize as his good manners kicking in. He was definitely humoring her.

The only thing to be done was to make matters worse.

"Cruz tells me you won't take his calls."

That didn't even earn the polite smile.

She forged ahead. "Seems like since he put his plane and his Jeep up for your bond, you'd at least talk to him."

"Not your business, Claire," he said, pushing away his plate, only half eaten.

"Probably not. But it's my job to make sure your life doesn't end up in shambles..."

"No," he interrupted, "it's your job to defend me in court. My life is already in shambles. If you do your job, then maybe, just maybe, I can put it all back together. But right now, the last thing I want to do is further alienate my only friends."

Brumby had often told her she didn't know when to leave well enough alone.

"And you think by not talking to them, you're not alienating them?"

He shrugged, suddenly deflated, looking tired and hopeless.

Back in the car. Back on the freeway.

"I'm sorry, Chris. You're right. It was none of my business."

He didn't even blink—very focused on the road ahead. Instead of being irritated at his silence, her heart went out to him. She resisted the urge to reach across and touch him.

"You don't have to do this alone, Chris. Your friends think the world of you and only want to help you. I know I'm just your attorney, but I'd like to think I'm your friend as well."

She let it go at that.

When they got back to the motel, he again opened her door and helped her out. He saw her safely to her room, all without comment.

At the door, she turned to face him.

"Thank you for dinner, Chris. I enjoyed being with you." And then, she did the unthinkable. She stood on tiptoe and placed a kiss on his cheek.

He froze.

And she froze.

Right there, staring at each other. Frozen on the edge of crumbling, of coming apart, of coming together.

Slowly, he stepped back, and put on the polite smile before turning and walking away.

She'd had plenty of kisses in her life, from the innocent ones when walked home by a boy who carried her books to the hot and steamy ones that left you panting and your insides reaching for more. But never had she had one that held more promise. She really liked this man. She could picture them being the best of friends for the rest of their lives, no matter how much distance lay between them.

Chris didn't have to try not to think as he drove home. He needed to work to focus, though. His eyes crossed more than once, and he gritted his teeth to concentrate on the road ahead.

Once home, he fell into bed, expecting to be dead to the world until his alarm sounded at five. That didn't happen. Instead, he tossed and turned, even got up once and puked. His hands shook.

In one corner of his brain, he clicked through every imaginable disease, taking inventory of how he felt. Eventually, he gave up, deciding that having your life crash around you might just have physical manifestations.

The only sweet spot in the night, which he spent up and down and only sleeping in small bits, was the kiss. Every defense he'd thrown up at her disapproval of his life choices and managed to keep up through dinner and the miserable trip home, had been weakened by her words, but had been completely undone by the kiss.

His stomach lurched with unshed tears.

He couldn't remember ever being so scared.

Chapter Fifteen

Chris didn't dread the list of crap job DQ would have waiting for him. He'd learned a long time ago that he could do anything, even clean up puke, blood and worse, once he just shut himself off from the task. DQ probably outdid himself with this list, though.

Whatever.

But he'd never walked into the Section before and not been part of it. Even at the worst of times, the Section was home.

Now, though, it was anything but.

Rooms that quieted when he entered.

The guys he'd laughed with, struggled with, saved, been saved by, no longer made eye contact with him. Or maybe he was unwilling to do so.

For the better part of the day, he managed to stay out of the way. He put up a *Wet Paint—Do Not Enter* sign at the door to the big storage room. He'd never thought about how big that room was. It took five hours to paint.

Then, he'd taken the ropes out back to examine them.

No one had come out to check on him.

Fine.

But, when Cruz walked past him in the hall and didn't even look up, Chris lost it.

He turned and fired the roll of two-inch tape he'd picked up on his way back inside, clocking Cruz in the back of the head.

"Christ," Cruz yelled, whirling around, ready to fight. "What the hell, Angel?"

That drew a crowd.

By then, Chris launched himself at his best friend and connected with Hollywood's precious face before he could react.

When Cruz did respond, he nailed Chris in the solar plexus, dropping him instantly. He lay curled in the hallway, fighting to breathe.

Minutes later, when he was finally able to move, Chris sat against the wall. Cruz was still doubled over, holding his bleeding nose.

A moment later, Cruz straightened and looked right at Gabe. Whatever he was about to say, he caught before it came out.

"Screw you, Gabriel," he said finally, stepped over Chris's outstretched legs, and headed for the front door, pushing past Will on his way.

"And screw you, too, Clancy."

"Me?" Clancy said, turning.

"Yeah, you're both lying dirt bags."

Will said nothing in return, only glancing briefly at Chris before returning to the dayroom. Nic came from the other end of the hall.

"Excuse me," he said when he, too, stepped over Chris. Then he followed Cruz out the front door.

"Gabriel," DQ said, from the doorway of his office, his voice tight, low, "go home."

"Sir?"

"I don't need this in my Section. Go home. I'll let you know when to come back."

Chris went home. But on his way, he stopped at City Hall to pick up the forms for a quitclaim deed. He had at least two hundred thousand dollars in equity in his building. He'd been making double payments since he bought it, and he'd been a bit lucky. With the recent downtown restoration project, the building had tripled in value. If Cruz owned his building, he could sell it for more than he'd invested in Gabe's freedom.

As soon as he got home, he filled out the papers and walked to a nearby office to get it notarized. Then he tucked it in an envelope with a note and mailed it.

That accomplished, he got in his car and drove to the only place he might—just might—still be welcome.

Claire checked her email one last time, then shut down her laptop. No more work for this day. Instead, she headed to a bookstore she'd seen yesterday, bought a biography of John Adams, and made a beeline for Denny's.

When he didn't see her in the pool, Chris went to her room and knocked. She didn't answer the door so he went back to the pool and sat in the late-afternoon sunshine. The warmth on his flight suit countered the slight chill in the breeze. The sun sparkled on the water in the pool, making him wish he'd brought his suit. He couldn't name the last time he'd gone swimming.

When she didn't show up by six, he pushed to his feet with a sigh and headed back to his apartment.

Will sat in a back corner at McGill's bar and downed a tequila before sipping the beer he'd ordered. He'd chosen this place because he had no real friends here. He could think about what he'd witnessed before he left work—his team torn apart.

Once Gabe left the Section, things had gradually lightened up a bit. Who was he kidding? Things had improved only slightly. Light was still a huge reach.

When Cruz came back in, accompanied by Nic, they were both laughing. But later, when Will came face-to-face with Cruz, he certainly wasn't laughing. Snarling, maybe. Laughing, not so much.

When he was no longer able to take it, Will had cornered Cruz in the vehicle bay.

"I had no choice, Hollywood."

"You always have a choice."

"Not this time. But I don't know anything that you don't already know."

At Cruz's skeptical look, Will assured him that was true.

Cruz was in no mood to talk.

"You knew he was screwing his best friend's wife?"

Nic moved in from across the room.

"He wasn't..." Will started, then stopped. Even if he hadn't been sworn to secrecy, his defense of Gabe, at this moment anyway, would have fallen on unwilling ears.

Now, Will took another draw on his beer.

Cruz's accusation wasn't true. That night, the pillows from the couch were stacked on the floor. Gabe was anal enough that this was a dead giveaway if you were paying attention. Gabe had been sleeping on the couch. Will knew it. Obviously, Cruz didn't. So there was something that Will knew that Cruz didn't.

But in order to set Cruz straight, he'd have to admit to being there. And Gabe was counting on him not to talk.

The lieutenant was counting on him to do the right thing.

Hard as it was to keep his mouth shut—and he still wasn't sure that was the right choice—the hardest thing was watching his team self-destruct.

Yoda was doing his best to hold the teams together. But the forces of the dark side were dead set against him.

Cruz and Gabe were at each other's throats. Nic was quiet—much more quiet than usual—keeping the peace where he could.

And Cowboy—when he realized he couldn't get a laugh to save his life, ducked off to the corner and stayed by himself.

Maybe now was a good time for a career move.

Cruz knew that if Clancy wasn't at the O, he'd be at McGill's. He liked hanging out in the dark corners, watching people. Even though he'd done a couple years in Air Force Intelligence, Clancy had taught him a lot about being observant. The guy noticed everything. If someone wore new socks, he'd notice. Clancy would make a good spy, except for his hesitance to break the law. Despite everything, Clancy was a wide-eyed innocent. He thought the good guys always won and still got miffed—miffed was a word Clancy would use—when things didn't turn out the way he thought they should. He was also an unmitigated romantic. Maybe those things just went together. Who knew?

Cruz entered McGill's tentatively at best. It was like swimming out beyond the sandbar where the sharks liked to hang out. You were fairly safe near the shore. The sharks didn't come in close. Much.

But out in the deeper water, you were definitely swimming at your own peril. That's what McGill's was—shark-infested territory. Maybe the sharks wouldn't be there now. Maybe he could get in and out without trouble.

Luckily, Kit wasn't there at this hour. But, as expected, Clancy was—in the back corner, nursing a Bud Light in a bottle and picking at nachos. Cruz knew Clancy saw him walk in but allowed him the space to be surprised to see him.

"*Una cervesa, por favor*," he said to Lynn, the usual waitress, "at Clancy's table."

Clancy didn't object when he sat down. Didn't say anything at all. Even after Lynn brought the Corona. It was obviously up to Cruz to break the silence.

He jumped in with both feet.

"How do you know Gabe didn't sleep with Max's wife?"

Clancy gave him a *you've-got-to-be-kidding* look.

"Okay. Let me rephrase that, since you still haven't decided that you'll do Gabe more favors if you talk. Are you absolutely positive that Gabe didn't screw Max's wife."

"No," Clancy said before lifting his gaze to the ceiling as he searched for words.

Cruz drank his beer and waited.

Clancy went on. "Why would you sleep on the couch if you were doing the girl who slept in your bed?"

"Point taken. And you *are* absolutely certain that he was sleeping on the couch?"

"Yes."

It was Cruz's turn to think. He sorted through what he knew and what he yet needed to know. He hated not being able to make the pieces fit.

"You told us Gabe was lying to you even before Max died, right?"

Clancy nodded, considering.

"Why was he lying even then, if he was sleeping on the couch?"

Finally, Clancy shrugged. "Maybe she asked him to."

A simple answer, but just might be the truth of it. Of course, it begged the question: Why would she not want anyone to know she was here?

"Clancy, do you know anyone at JAG headquarters in Washington?"

"Not as well as you obviously do."

Not only bright and observant, but witty as well. He must have seen Cruz talking to Claire.

"*Touché*. We need more information, Clancy." With that, he reached over and swiped a chip, loaded with cheese.

"Take the best ones, Hollywood."

"I always do, little Will. I always do."

Claire returned to her room after a slow dinner. She ate while she read. She drank way too much iced tea and now sat on the motel bed, wired, nearly bouncing, as she watched Headline News.

She refused to check email again or even crack her laptop. Work was over for the day. That left her buzzed and way too open to the longing to see Chris. She'd managed to keep it at bay all day by working. Now, she was vulnerable. Not a position she liked.

Flipping to the hotel movie guide, she found a spy movie that looked like it might do the job. It didn't, but she wasn't sure she wanted to admit that.

Chris was up, drinking Pepsi and tearing up flooring by six. He tried to eat, but his stomach rebelled. He was getting sick, but was powerless to do anything. For a moment, he considered calling the unit's physician adviser, getting a prescription. But for what? Sleep, maybe. Nausea, maybe. Anti-anxiety, not on your life.

God, he was pitiful.

He hated pitiful.

By God, he would not be pitiful.

So here he was, tearing up the last row of planks—harder than laying them he learned—then planning the rest of the day. If he could get the floor done, he could move on to the bathroom upgrades. Once those were done, he could paint, and Cruz would have himself another income stream.

Like he needed one.

Claire couldn't come up with a reason to visit her client. Well, not an official one. And going over there just to go over there was pathetic and needy. Maybe she could just say she was there to check how he was.

He'd see right through that.

And she was the one that planted the silly little kiss. A shiver of regret went up her spine, followed closely by the incessant longing that had taken root inside.

Work. She needed to work. She had five days until the prelim. Maybe Brumby had news. Maybe Cruz had news. Maybe she should just go by the apartment.

"Captain Janova," she said to her reflection in the motel mirror. "You need to straighten up. Knock off the romance stuff. Pause for a moment, and orient yourself."

The only problem was that Chris Gabriel had suddenly become true north.

At noon, Chris heard someone on the steps. He was hot and sweaty and not in the mood for a visitor. That changed, though when he saw who it was.

"Julie. Hi."

She smiled broadly and tucked her blonde hair behind her ear, then moved her sunglasses onto her head like a headband.

She hugged him.

It felt so good, he nearly cried.

And she hung on, sniffling once or twice. Then she leaned back, her hands still on his waist.

"How are you, Angel?"

He tried to say *okay*, but the word couldn't make it past the lump in his throat. When he couldn't answer, she moved back into the hug, and he held her tight. They stood there like that until her phone rang. She stepped back to answer, a smile playing on her lips.

"Hi babe." It was Nic. "I'm over at Angel's. Why?"

She listened, nodded.

"Oh, well, I actually brought food for us, so I guess I'll take a rain check."

The conversation ended, and she tossed her phone into her bag.

It was almost like nothing was going on. For a moment, Chris wondered if she even knew.

They chatted for a few minutes, not yet getting to the food, before more steps down the hall announced another arrival.

Nic came through the open door and stopped, obviously at a loss for words. The tension in the room was tangible, so Chris put a stop to it.

"You know, Julie, I just ate a little while ago," Chris said. Six weeks ago, he wouldn't have even considered this kind of lie. "So, you and Nic take the food to the park, and have a great lunch. Thanks for coming by."

Julie's eyes narrowed. She looked at Nic, then back at Chris.

"Actually," she said, bending to pick up both the food and her bag, "maybe I'll go eat alone. Take care, Angel. If you need me, call."

With another quick look at Nic, and a shake of her head, she left. Nic lowered his gaze for a moment before, without a word, he followed her out.

Chris checked his watch. Unless Nic was just around the corner when he called her, he'd made it here from the Section in record time.

To save his beloved from his friend.

For the first time, disappearing didn't sound half bad.

In just over an hour, Eric had pulled off the best takeover of his life. Not the first or the biggest, dollarwise. But certainly the most amazing. Hostile? Maybe just a bit. But she'd get over it. Time to celebrate. Maybe the Thursday night poker game was still going on.

Cruz looked around the half-full bar, but Clancy was gone. The bartender—a relative newbie named Jeff or John or something—said that Clancy had been there but had left a little while ago. No one else had shown. The Thursday night game had been a bust.

"No mission going on?" the bartender asked.

"No mission."

"So what's up with that?"

"Good question. Give me a stout."

If it weren't nearing ten, he'd call Red and see if she wanted a beer. The news would have to wait until

JAX HUNTER

Saturday.

Chapter Sixteen

On Friday afternoon, the Section had visitors. Will was the first to greet them as he was standing outside when they arrived.

"Colonel," Will said as they approached the front door. The colonel was retired, teaching at the Academy as a civilian. He looked great—hardly limped—and Lily, well, she just looked completely happy. Will couldn't bring himself to call him anything other than colonel—well, maybe Mac.

"Clancy," Mac reached forward and shook Will's hand. "How goes it?"

Will glanced over at DQ, who was with them, but he couldn't tell if the lieutenant had filled the colonel in or not.

"Good, sir. Fine. Ma'am," he said to Lily, "it's good to see you. We heard that you two snuck off to the Caymans to get married. Congratulations."

"Thank you, Will," she said, then smiled at her husband. "Will you be at the party tomorrow?"

"Yes, ma'am. We all will be."

"Good, we'll see you then. And Clancy?"

"Yes, ma'am?"

"You can drop the *ma'am*."

"Yes...oh, okay."

The reception inside—Will followed them in—was hearty and happy. Mac was his usual self, cutting up.

"Where's Gabe?' Mac said at last.

The room got utterly still.

DQ cleared his throat.

The clock ticked.

Then, finally, the lieutenant put his head down and sighed.

"Guess we need to talk, sir."

The threesome trudged into the lieutenant's office, and once again, the door closed.

Chris was sitting on the patio of the coffee shop across the street from his apartment.

His first instinct, when he saw them, was to get up and greet them happily. But he didn't. Instead, he ducked his head and let Mac and Lily think he wasn't home.

Claire hadn't talked to her client since yesterday morning. She'd called the Section to be transferred to the lieutenant, who told her about the near brawl in his building and that he'd sent the Champ home to cool his jets. She then called Chris's cell and reached him.

He'd been short and direct. He was staying busy in the apartment next door. He didn't need anything. Underneath his abrupt tone, though, Claire thought she heard a hopelessness that seemed to be getting worse.

She called Cruz.

He hadn't talked to Gabe. Had quit trying, actually.

"I'm concerned about him. Is he always this alone, Cruz?"

"He likes his privacy."

"Okay, but..."

"Is he coming to the hail and farewell tomorrow night? He does great in crowds."

She got the details in case Chris didn't have them, but waited to call him back.

"Hello," he answered.

"Even broody champions need to eat."

"I'm not hungry." At least he didn't say he wasn't broody.

"Tough, I'll pick you up in fifteen. Get dressed. Dinner's on me. How's the food at the pizza place just north of your house?"

"Never been there."

"Good. We'll be guinea pigs together."

When she got there, he was out front, leaning against the building. He looked dreadful—almost as bad as when they'd picked him up from the jail. If a person could lose weight in days, he was doing it. He didn't really have it to lose. His face was drawn, and to say he had dark circles under his eyes, would be a vast understatement.

"C'mon, Champ," she said after rolling down the passenger side window.

He slowly pushed away from the wall and walked to her car.

"I told you, I'm not hungry," he said, pulling the door closed.

"Humor me, Chris."

"No one calls me Chris."

She glanced over, trying to read his expression.

"Do you not like it?"

He was slow in answering. "No, it's fine."

The food was just okay, but she convinced him to eat a slice of pizza—well, almost a whole slice.

"Are you sleeping, Chris?"

He shrugged.

"Do we need to get you a prescription?"

"No, we don't. I'll be fine."

"Okay, then. But you need to sleep and you need to eat. I'd like you to look human at the prelim."

He fixed her with an annoyed look, but said nothing.

"You going to your colonel's hail and farewell tomorrow night?"

"Wasn't planning on it. Not sure I'm especially welcome."

She pulled her phone and the card with the home phone written on the back from her purse. She dialed.

"Lieutenant? Claire Janova here."

The look on his face jumped from annoyed to downright hostile.

"Just checking to see if Gabriel is welcome at the party tomorrow night. I'll be there to chaperone him."

"Can you keep him in line, ma'am?"

"Yes, Lieutenant, I can. Thank you."

She hung up, then turned to Gabe. "So, pick me up at six thirty, and dress nice. We'll go say farewell to your colonel."

He didn't respond—didn't even shrug—just looked away.

When she pulled in to drop him off, he didn't get out.

"What are our chances, Claire?"

The worst thing a defense attorney could do was not prepare her client for the reality that they might lose. To overstate their case and make bald-faced guarantees would be like leaving a man to bleed on the sidewalk and tell him he was going to be fine. He was a lawyer, so he knew that. He also knew she'd level with him.

"With another attorney, I'd say fair. But I'm not another attorney, so I'll say fifty-fifty."

When he moved to get out of the car, she reached for his arm. "Call me at midnight if you're awake."

Grey eyes locked with hers as he considered her words.

"Do I need to order you to call, Champ?"

"No. If I'm awake, I'll call. Thanks for dinner."

When she got back to her room, the message light was flashing.

"Claire," Chris's voice, "thanks for taking this case. I appreciate all your hard work on my behalf."

She could hear his voice go all husky at the end, and tears clogged her own throat.

"I won't let you down, Chris."

At seven minutes after midnight, Chris gave up the battle and dialed the phone.

"You can't sleep, either?" she said when she picked up the phone.

"Not for weeks, it seems."

"Where are you?"

He smiled—it came hard. "Is that like *what are you wearing?*

She laughed. "No, I just wondered if you were in bed."

"That doesn't sound much better, Captain."

"I'm thinking that attorney-client relationship doesn't include phone sex, Champ."

He laughed. "That's all right. I have a headache."

"Really?"

"For weeks, it seems."

"You want to come swim in my pool?" she said.

"It's not closed for the night?"

"It's not locked. What are they going to do, throw us in jail for swimming after midnight? I know a good lawyer or two. We'll be out in five on good behavior."

"I'll meet you there in fifteen minutes. And Claire, be quiet about it."

In the end, they didn't swim much after the first burst of frustration had them racing. She was good. He was better.

Then, they sat on the steps in the pool—the water was warmer than the air—and talked.

He told her about the pipeline. She'd been unfamiliar with the nickname.

"It's a succession of schools for pararescue—Superman School. Let's see. Indoc. Airborne. Combat Diver. Underwater Egress." He enumerated on his fingers. "Basic Survival. Freefall. Combat Medic. Recovery Specialist. We had to swim two thousand meters in open water in BDUs, drown proof. You name it, we did it. Few of us got through without drowning at least once."

"I've heard you guys are actually better trained than SEALs."

"Don't let a SEAL hear you say that."

"I gotta say, Sergeant, I'm duly impressed."

He took her hand. The warmth that surged through him at the small act surprised him.

"Nic felt it necessary to rescue his fiancée from me."

Claire was so distracted by his taking her hand, she almost missed his statement. But the sadness that filled his soft voice—almost a whisper, in fact, to keep from waking the other guests—nearly made her cry. She pulled their hands up from the water and kissed the back of his hand.

"I'm so sorry, Champ."

They sat in silence for a time.

"You want me to kick his ass?" She so wanted to see him smile.

He did, but the smile was small and gloomy.

"You know, Sergeant, we're in pretty iffy waters here."

"Really? Not enough chlorine?"

She peeked over at him. He was looking at her from the corner of his eye, not turning his head.

"Oh, my God, you made a joke!" she whispered, momentarily putting her head on his shoulder.

"Not much of one. And, yes, we are in iffy waters. But I can't quite make myself care."

"I'm with you there."

His turn to kiss the back of her hand before launching out into the water. For ten minutes he swam, length after length, slicing through the water like a knife, with hardly a ripple, hardly a sound.

Once out of the water, they sat in lounge chairs side by side, not touching, still whispering.

"It's a little cold," Claire said, thinking maybe she should go get blankets. The alternative was to see if he wanted to come in—and that was such a bad idea.

He didn't answer.

When she looked over, she realized that he was asleep.

Quietly, she went back to her room, threw on her sweats and got the blankets.

Saturday, dawn, she still sat beside him, watching over him as he slept.

Nothing had happened.

And yet, everything had changed.

The girl was wearing silk. Silk. What was up with that? Cruz gritted his teeth and reminded himself that he had the upper hand here, even though, at the moment, it didn't much feel like it.

After all, he wouldn't be picking her up if he truly had the upper hand. How the red-haired wench always got her way peeved the hell out of him.

Before he knew what was happening, he was out of the car and holding the door for her.

He did that only for chicks he really dug, chicks he wanted to get into bed.

"No," he growled.

"Excuse me?" Kit asked?

He hadn't meant that to come out.

"Nothing. You look nice."

"Knock it off, Hotshot. We're not on a date."

"I know."

For having the upper hand, he was sure floundering. He drove in silence to the Club.

"I thought they said this was at the Officer's Club," she said as he pulled into the parking lot.

He laughed.

"No, just the Club. No Officer's Club here, not a big-enough outfit. But this place is the O Club when needed and the NCO Club when needed. It's pretty nice. Great patio out back. Gazebo, trees, flowers. All overlooking a great—if man-made—lake."

For a moment, walking in with Kit Sheridan on his arm, Cruz actually found himself feeling something akin to pride.

He'd have the hottest woman in the room.

If she'd stay with him.

Since waking up this morning with the sun on his face, with Claire sitting beside him, hugging her knees to her chest, her dark hair hanging soft down her back, Chris felt almost human again.

Almost hopeful.

She'd looked over at him and smiled.

"Morning, Champ," she'd said.

At that moment, he knew he wanted to hear those words from her every day for the rest of his life.

Having her beside him—even if she were clear across the country—sounded like paradise.

Someone to talk to.

Someone to not talk to.

Someone who was smart and beautiful and independent, who understood that two people could be one without sucking the life out of each other.

Crazy.

Yet, here he was, hours later, walking to her room to get her, hoping that she'd like his sweater.

Silly.

He knocked on her door, and when she smiled at him, his life was complete.

Despite being charged with murder and having his friends all think he was guilty.

"Tell me about your colonel," Claire asked on the way.

"He was a great commander. We all loved him, trusted him. He has integrity. Oh, and a bizarre sense of humor. He just retired, what, about a month ago. He crashed his helicopter on a mission in February. He met Lily, and they eloped in Grand Cayman on their way to Colorado."

"Grand Cayman isn't on the way to Colorado," she said.

"For them, it was."

Kit was among good company, if Eric could just relax and live in the moment.

Lily—the other redhead in the room—looked beautiful. Marriage to the colonel must agree with her. She hugged Cruz when she saw him and thanked him for playing cupid. At that, Kit just shook her head. He grinned.

Kit had been present when Cruz did his latest stint as Cupid—she'd told him not to give up his day job.

"See, I did good that night," Cruz said.

Kit leaned close and whispered right in his ear, "That's not how I remember it."

That same night, he'd fled from Kit's place just when things were getting interesting. This was the first time she'd actually mentioned it.

Eric didn't realize that he was capable of blushing. Yet, here he was, brought low by this woman.

Still, all he could think of was getting the speeches and gift giving out of the way so he could get her alone and kiss her.

When he looked up, though, Kit was introducing herself to the other gorgeous woman in the room, who seemed very much at ease with her client.

"Gabe."

"Cruz."

Despite Claire's presence beside him, Chris felt very much like a lost school boy. He stood face-to-face with his best friend, and he couldn't find words.

The best he could do was to clear his throat.

When Cruz asked why he'd sent the quitclaim deed, Chris could only shrug.

When he came face-to-face with Mac and Lily, he couldn't do more than mumble that it was nice to see them.

And when the room started to close in on him, he made his way out back, gulping in lungfuls of air in an effort to stay on his feet.

Chapter Seventeen

Claire watched him flee. She stayed and talked with the colonel for a moment until he was drawn away by a man who might have been a general.

"You're Angel's attorney?"

It was the colonel's wife.

"That's right. Claire Janova."

"Claire, I'm Lily. You've known him from before all this, then?"

"Who? Chris? No, I just met him a few days ago."

"Hmm." Now the girl—well, not a girl really, but significantly younger than the colonel—smiled as if she knew something Claire didn't. "Well, I hope you can get to the truth and get our Angel out of trouble."

Our Angel. The way Lily said it seemed like she referred to she and Claire, not to she and her colonel.

Claire looked toward the back door and wondered if their *Angel* was okay.

"Excuse me," she said to Lily.

"You'll take good care of him, Claire?"

"Yes, Lily, I will."

When she got out back, she found Chris talking with Nic, so she stepped back inside the door.

But just inside the door.

When Will saw the serious looks on Nic and Gabe's faces, he changed his mind about going outside. That explained the captain standing inside as well. He turned and ran square into the colonel's wife.

"Sorry, ma'am," he said before catching himself. "Hi, Lily. You might not want to go out there, Nic and Gabe are engaged in what looks to be an uncomfortable conversation."

She smiled and slipped her hand into the crook of his arm.

"Well, then Clancy, I guess we'll have to peruse the food. C'mon."

She steered him to the appetizers. Once they'd filled plates, they moved over to a corner to sit.

"So, how are things, really?"

Lily didn't miss much, and she really seemed to care about those around her. She was the classic nurturing soul.

"They're rough at the moment."

"I can see that. Mac made a phone call and assures me Captain Janova is a good lawyer."

"Seems to be." Again, he had to bite off the ma'am at the end. "How are you liking Colorado Springs?"

"It's a nice city. We rented a place over on the west side. They tell me it's where all the old hippies hang out. But we're planning to build a house on the south end, in the shadow of Cheyenne Mountain. It's further for Mac to drive to the Academy, but I've sort of bonded with the mountain."

"Good. I'm glad things are going well."

The band, who'd been on a short break, started up again. A few people made their way out onto the dance floor. Will set his plate on a nearby table and brushed the crumbs from his slacks.

"Mac misses you all. If he had something to do here, I think it wouldn't take much to get him back," Lily said.

"He should talk to Kit. Maybe she's hiring. How's Daniel?"

Daniel had just started back to work, and none of the PJs had actually talked to him.

"Not great, Clancy. He says he's fine, but he's not one to ever complain. I have a hunch he's as good as he's going to get."

"I'm sorry to hear that."

"Hi, gorgeous," Mac said as he held out his hand to Lily. "The higher-ups want to see if I've abused you in any way. Care to show them that I remain a gentleman and a scholar?"

"A gentleman and a scholar?" she said, giving him one of those special smiles that couples share.

"Fine. A gentleman."

She placed her hand in his, and he tugged her to her feet, then embraced her briefly—very briefly.

"Well, sir," Will said, standing, "it appears that any chance of any of us stealing her away from you are slim to none."

"You got that right, Clancy."

The twosome wandered off. Will joined Cowboy, who stood forlorn in the corner near the bar.

Nic caught up with Chris in mid-gulp, bending over, hands on his knees, trying hard not to hurl.

"You okay, Angel?" Nic asked, then stepped back a bit, giving him room to get his act together.

Chris nodded and straightened.

"I think you should present the picture to Mac," Nic said.

"Why?"

"Because you're the one that came up with the idea. You're the one that ran everyone down to sign it."

Chris looked over at Nic, who stood, hands in pockets, glancing out at the flowers down the path. He sounded sincere, but looked unhappy to say the least.

Get past the bullshit.

"Why did you feel you had to protect Julie from me? Did you really think I'd hurt her...or that I'd have sex with her?"

"What?"

"Answer the question, Nic."

"What the hell are you talking about?"

Nic really didn't know what he was talking about.

"Never mind."

"No, this is bullshit. What are you talking about, Gabe?" Nic's voice was getting higher, like it did when he was really upset.

"The other day, when Julie came by to see me. You came charging in to save her from me."

Nic frowned. Really frowned, like Gabe hadn't see him frown for a very long time.

"When I came to get Julie the other day it was because..."

Nic's tone, more than his words, dropped a stone right in Gabe's gut. He knew Batman's next words even before Nic managed to get them out.

"I got orders for Afghanistan."

"Oh, Nic. No."

The last Bravo Squad member that went TDY to the Middle East came back in a casket. Joey was Nic's best friend from childhood. And his death had nearly destroyed Batman.

"We didn't want to ruin the party."

Chris turned to see Julie and Claire standing in the doorway.

Julie moved over to stand with Nic. Claire stayed put.

"We'll make the announcement tomorrow," Julie said, taking Nic's arm and laying her cheek on him. "We're throwing together a small wedding. On Wednesday evening. Nic leaves Friday."

Her voice wavered and she looked up at Nic. She pressed her lips together, fighting back tears.

"I was hoping, since my dad is gone that you'd give me away, Angel."

Claire watched Chris struggle with Julie's words, with the emotion that seemed to overwhelm all of them. But there, before her eyes, he seemed to gain strength. He raised up, standing to his full glorious height, and smiled. Not the polite-Gabe smile, but the real thing.

He leaned over and kissed Julie on the top of her head.

"I'd be honored, sweetheart. And, Nic, I'd be glad to do the honors today. Thank you."

Julie was in tears, and Claire was close.

Nic nodded. When he was able to speak, "We'll be back in a few, and we can make the presentation." He put his arm around Julie and steered her down the path.

Claire joined Chris as Nic and Julie disappeared from view. Despite the rules and the risk, she slipped her hand into his.

The moment only lasted a moment before a cleared throat announced the arrival of Colonel McIntyre. Claire withdrew, but not before squeezing his hand.

"Excuse me, Colonel. I need to powder my nose," she said, leaving her champion to talk with his champion.

"Your attorney, huh?" Mac said without even trying to hide the mischief in his voice.

"Yes, sir," Chris said with his own smile.

"Good luck with that, Gabe."

"Thank you, sir. And congratulations on your marriage."

"Thanks. Can you believe she actually married me? And you guys didn't *sir* me before, so don't start now."

"Okay. How's life at the Academy, then?"

"Good, I guess. I'm not sure I'm cut out to be a teacher, but since it's just Military Studies, they're not expecting much."

Gabe laughed. It was well known in the Air Force that, if you weren't qualified to teach anything else, you could always teach Military Studies. At least having Mac for a professor, you wouldn't fall asleep. Laughing, maybe. Sleeping, never. He'd throw something at you if you did.

"Does Lily like the Springs? Claire's from there originally."

"Claire?"

"Captain Janova."

Mac laughed. "Hang in there, Gabe." The colonel paused, concern gave way to assurance. "I'm sure it will all work out."

"God, I hope so, sir."

"We believe in you, Batman." Mac slapped him on the back then headed back inside.

The fourth gorgeous woman at the shindig came in with her superhero, but she looked like she'd been crying. Actually, said superhero looked a bit like he'd been crying as well. Before Cruz could ponder long what could be wrong, Gabe called for everyone's attention.

Wow, he was actually smiling.

"Colonel, the last time we tried to do this, we all had to go to work without you. Though Colonel Scott is adequate," he nodded and smiled politely at their new commander, "we still miss you. And since now you have a whole bunch of kids to look after, and you might forget your kids here, we got you this to remember us by."

Gabe turned and picked up the wrapped frame and handed it to Scarecrow.

Mac ripped the paper from the present and stood, stunned, looking at the picture.

"Is this my bird?"

"Yes, sir, with you at the stick."

"No kidding?"

It was a great photo, of Leroy Zero Eight as the colonel pulled it close to the drogue of the King Bird to refuel in midair. The process was intricate, and Eric had never flown with another pilot that did it so well.

"Wow," Kit said, awestruck.

Eric had been so engrossed in the proceedings that he hadn't noticed.

Kit was almost as mesmerized as Mac was.

Each member of the squadron had signed the matte, and there was a listing on the back of all the men that had come through the unit while Mac was commanding. Joey Amonte was the only one that was not alive today, and that certainly was through no lack of leadership on Mac's part.

"Thank you, all. I'll treasure it," Mac said, his voice slightly gruff. "You guys always made me look good. You don't have a problem, Tom," he said to the new commander, "if I borrow them once in a while in the Springs. I need all the help I can get."

Everyone laughed a bit uncomfortably, and the moment passed.

There were speeches from the general and the new colonel—highly unusual for a hail and farewell, outgoing and incoming hardly ever even acknowledged one another—but Cruz had tuned the whole thing out and was now fully focused on the task at hand.

He turned off his better judgment and went in for the kill.

"Are you ready for Monday or do you have to work tomorrow?" Chris asked as he walked Claire to her room.

"I'm ready. You?"

"I'd rather pretend that nothing's happening Monday morning. And, since you don't have to work, can I take you to the park tomorrow?"

"Okay."

He hadn't expected her to object but the ease with which she answered surprised him.

"Good. I'll pick you up at ten, then. Wear sturdy shoes."

"For the park?"

"Not the park, Claire. *The* park."

At her look of confusion, he shook his head.

"You'll see," he said and leaned in to kiss her.

He got stuck about an inch from her lips. Her eyes didn't leave his, and they held everything he wanted to see there: challenge, humor, warmth, and maybe just a touch of seduction. It took his breath away.

Instead of pulling back, though, like he should have, he stayed right there. She came the rest of the way.

Her lips were warm and soft. Yielding. If he wanted to, he could have pressed the advantage. He wanted to. But he was content not to. He pulled back and smiled.

"Thanks for today, Claire."

"You're welcome, Chris."

They walked hand in hand in the shadow of one of the most famous natural walls in the world.

"Please tell me that you don't need flowers and romantic walks on the beach, Claire," Chris said.

She laughed. "Not much into romance, Champ?"

"Not much."

"Yet, here you are."

He stopped walking and steered her to turn around.

"Maybe, but there are kites in the car."

"Well," Claire said, pulling him along toward the car, "roses are okay, but kites? Show me."

And he did just that. The first kite he pulled out was pretty simple.

"The days of running to get them airborne is long past," he said. "Just throw it up and tug on the string a bit."

Amazingly, that worked. Soon, the little kite was played out to its length of string, and they sat on a rock and watched it fly. At that point, it took only an occasional tug to keep it flying.

"It's a beer kite."

"A beer kite?"

"Yeah, you can fly it with one hand and drink a beer with the other."

The next kite was like nothing she'd ever seen before, though admittedly, she was pretty much a kite rookie.

Chris was in his element. Apparently, he'd been flying kites on the beaches of Florida since high school.

"Trying to impress the girls?"

"Yeah, right. More like a way to assuage the pain of rejection."

This kite was huge, with two strings attached to substantial handles. It looked like it took all his strength to fly it.

"Well, I'm impressed. I won't even ask to fly this one."

"I thought you were adventurous, Captain."

"I am, Sergeant."

"Then step in here between my arms, and I'll let you have the helm."

Claire didn't need more encouragement. She ducked under his right arm and backed up against him. She slipped her hands into the straps, if that's what they were called. He didn't give her control, though, his hands enveloping hers. From the strong pull from the monster, she was glad for that.

The sun had warmed her hair, her skin. She smelled good. Chris had felt so comfortable with her that, until this moment, he'd been able to ignore the desire rippling under the surface. Well, almost ignore it. More like let it simmer.

That was impossible at the moment.

If he'd have been able to let go of the straps and really let her fly the kite, he'd have slipped his hands around her, maybe kissed the side of her neck...

But he couldn't let go, not unless he wanted the drag to pull her off her feet.

He'd seen someone scudded along the beach before by a kite, before finally letting go, allowing the kite to crash. But this wasn't the beach. She could get hurt.

As if sensing his thoughts, she moved forward, so they weren't touching.

"Take them, Chris," she said over her shoulder.

He did, and she ducked away.

The perplexed look on her flushed face told him that she was fighting it, too. He wanted to say something, to talk about it, but couldn't get the words to form.

It seemed to be a constant state of affairs between them. Either he wouldn't talk to her, or he couldn't. And yet, it was almost as if he didn't need to.

Claire watched from a safe distance as Chris let the kite play a while longer, and the conversation began again, haltingly. Soon, though, they were talking again about his days on the beach in Florida.

"What does it say under your yearbook picture—*boy most likely to throw away his commission to become a rock jock?*"

He eased his gaze over to her, then back up at the kite. Could she please have her mouth sewn shut? She'd never been a babbler. Actually, she'd always had fairly decent control over what came out of her mouth. Until now.

"That really bugs you, doesn't it? I didn't take you for an elitist."

She could only shake her head.

"I'm sorry."

He glanced at her again and gave her one of the Gabe-smiles. She'd come to think of it as a mask that he slid into place when it was required by the rules of courtesy.

Instantly, she decided she never wanted to be the recipient of *that* smile again. She wanted only real smiles from him—the kind that made her shiver.

She didn't explain, was afraid she'd just make it worse if she did. But then, she didn't want him to think she didn't respect his position.

"I am sorry, Chris. I didn't mean that to be a slam. I can't say that I understand your decision, but I do not think less of you for it."

"No matter. My father said the same thing."

Chris started reeling in the kite without further conversation. Soon, they were winding their way back through the park the way they came.

"Come to the pool?" Claire asked in a squeaky voice—odd for her—as Chris pulled into the motel parking lot.

"I don't have my suit with me."

"You want to...um, go get it?"

She was asking more than if he wanted to swim.

He very much wanted to swim.

He'd never wanted to swim so much in his life.

Yet, he was not willing to risk the way they were together.

"Claire, I..."

"It's okay. Don't..."

"Claire..." Chris got out of the car and walked around, helping her. Then, he took her perfect face in his hands and kissed her. "I would love to make love to you. If I knew that what we have wasn't fragile... I just don't want to risk..."

"Chris," she said, looking up at him.

The heat in her gaze nearly driving him to his knees.

"What we have is not at all fragile. Go get your suit."

He let his hands slide down her face, her neck, then her shoulders.

"If you change your mind before I get back, call my cell," he said.

"I won't."

As he took the stairs to his apartment three at a time, his phone rang.

"Change your mind?"

"Sort of." Her voice was silken and his body stiffened in response. "Skip the swim. Come to my room, Chris."

He laughed uncomfortably.

"How about this? I'll meet you at the pool in twenty minutes. We'll see if reason returns. If not, we have all evening to go to your room."

She didn't speak for a moment, and he flashed back to Suzanne and her fury at his rejection. He wasn't rejecting Claire, though.

"Chris?" Silken and sultry.

"Yes?"
Again, a long silence.
"I'll see you at the pool."
"You will indeed."
On his way back down to the car, he snagged a bottle of Chardonnay and two glasses.

Chapter Eighteen

Reason did return, sort of.

The smoldering they'd managed to control had flared when they flew the kite together, then was fanned by her voice on the phone. Now, when she smiled up at him as he peeled off his shirt and dove into the water, fire surged through his veins, making it hard to breath.

He slipped up before her and slicked the water from his face. Up close, it was obvious she felt the fire, too. Her lips parted.

"You brought wine?"

"Yes."

She raised her hands and trailed her fingertips down his chest.

In self-defense, he tugged her hands away, pulling them to his mouth. She had elegant hands, long, slim fingers with neatly trimmed nails, no polish.

He kept his eyes locked on hers and tried desperately to get his body to slow down.

Claire couldn't remember ever aching this way. She couldn't think. Never had propriety and sound judgment so completely deserted her. All she could do—all she *wanted* to do—was to allow the raging currents to sweep her away—sweep them both away. She simply could not get enough of this man.

Pressed against each other, their eyes locked. They were two people with one thought, one focus. With an abandon she'd never even considered before, she took her hands from his and pulled him in to her lips.

He groaned, then tangled his hands in her wet hair, devouring her with his mouth.

And reason slammed into her like a freight train.

"Stop."

He did. No balking. She didn't have to ask twice. He simply stepped back.

"I know. I feel it, too. Let's catch our breath, maybe dry off, have a glass of wine."

He wasn't angry, didn't even seem upset. He smiled, his grey eyes soft. Grey eyes she loved. The man she loved.

They were stuck there for a moment before she finally spoke.

"Back to my room? Or not?"

He grinned. "Anything good on TV?"

"Probably not."

"You go on, get some dry clothes on. I'll be there in a bit."

At that, he launched into the deep end. Claire watched him glide silently through the water, turn and go again. She picked up her towel and the wine and headed inside. He was still doing laps when she stepped through the door.

Fifteen minutes later, he knocked softly. She opened it to find him dressed in jeans and a t-shirt, his hair still wet.

They sat on the bed and drank the wine, found a baseball game to watch, and talked. When the wine was gone, Chris flipped off the TV, turned off the light, and pulled her into his arms. And they slept, spoon fashion, fit together as if they were made for each other. Fully clothed.

At two twenty-three, reality hit. The light from the street snuck through the gap in the curtains and touched on his perfect face, now relaxed in sleep. Sweet lips, a strong, straight nose, a single lock of dark hair falling onto his forehead.

The worry he carried, even the first time she saw him, the worry that kept sleep away, kept him unable to eat, was momentarily eased from his features, and he looked younger.

She moved from the bed, afraid, somehow, her sudden plunge from euphoria would wake him.

He needed to sleep.

Tears came in earnest as she lowered herself to the chair and turned, unable to look at Chris, sleeping in her bed.

What if she failed?

If she failed, he'd be convicted of murder.

If she failed...

Oh, God.

A band of panic encircled her chest, making even the shallowest of breaths hard to pull in.

The voice of reason, which she'd tried desperately to put out of her misery, was loudly reminding her why there were rules against lawyers getting personally involved with their clients.

It wasn't good for the client.

An attorney that wasn't on top of her game could ruin her client's future, maybe even take his life.

Chris wasn't up on capital charges.

But that didn't lessen the horror of being found guilty.

Tears washed her face, and her hands shook.

And, for the first time in her career, she fervently doubted her ability to continue.

Chris lay perfectly still, listening to her cry.

His first thought had been that she was regretting their growing relationship. He loved her and didn't want her to regret that. But he knew, deep down, that wasn't it.

He drew in a deep breath.

"Suzanne showed up on Saturday, two weeks ago."

From her chair across the room, she listened to him tell the story.

"I loved her, Claire, but Max moved first. At least, I thought I loved her."

He let that thought hang in the air for a moment before continuing. Things unsaid were loud and clear.

He'd promised Suzanne that he would tell no one she was here. She was up and down and all over the place.

One minute, she'd be pouting over him rejecting her, and the next, over the moon about something or other. Somehow he'd missed classic symptoms of manic-depression. He blamed himself for that.

She'd suggested that Max was out to get her, implied that he would hurt her if he found her there.

Chris had tried to get ahold of her medical records to check.

"I'm not the best liar, I guess," he said, making Claire smile. Fact was, he was the worst liar she'd ever seen.

"The guy wouldn't send me her records and threatened to turn me in."

On Thursday morning, he'd broken his word to her and called Max, had second thoughts, and hung up before Max answered.

On Thursday night, he couldn't face going home to her and got a room at the Lazy 8 Motel.

"Would they verify that?" she interrupted, suddenly jazzed.

"Probably." He cleared his throat and continued. "I wasn't there very long. We got called out in the middle of the night."

When he got home from the mission, with Clancy on his heels, he found the door to his house open. Max was dead. Suzanne was gone. He'd sworn Clancy to silence as well.

"Poor Will," she said, now recognizing the agony Clancy had been in—not just from her, but from his teammates as well.

"I called Suz numerous times, left messages. Even spoke with her parents. She hasn't called back except when you talked to her."

There was a long silence.

"I guess I didn't want to think that she'd killed Max. I didn't want to disbelieve her. If there really is someone else involved, I didn't want to lead him to her."

"Loyalty," she said into the silence.

She could hear him move from the bed, but didn't look back.

"Misplaced loyalty?"

"I don't know, Chris."

"Claire."

"Hmmm?"

He moved up behind her, his fingers on her shoulders.

"I slept on the couch."

"I know."

"You do?"

She stood and moved to him, laying her head against his chest, wrapping her arms around his waist. His heart beat against her cheek, slow and steady.

"That same loyalty would have kept you from taking another man's wife, even if you had wanted to."

"How do you know that?"

"Because you're a champion."

Now he held her away, looking down at her quizzically, a small smile playing on his lips. "Where did you get that champion thing?"

"From your biggest fans."

"I didn't know I had any."

"Yes, you do."

She reached up and touched his face, a bit afraid she shouldn't, delighted that she could, then took his hand and drew him to the bed. Again, they lay together, talking.

From her position, her head on his shoulder, she told him what she knew about Suzanne's time in Iraq, her speculation that something had drastically changed as a result and about her suspicions that Suzanne was under a psychiatrist's care.

Finally, wrapped in each other, they slept again.

"I'll meet you at IHOP," he said as he opened the door to leave. God, he hated to go.

"I'll get dressed, and see you there at eight thirty."

Claire was keyed up, not in a bad way, rather excited about the prospects of proving his whereabouts on Thursday night. He couldn't quite imagine how *on* she'd be after a plate filled with carbs, smothered in sugar. But he couldn't wait to see.

The little he'd seen of her in action—dressed in uniform, so serious, so confident—just made him want to see more. Even if he hadn't been a little bit in love with her—who was he kidding, he was completely in love with her—he'd be intrigued at the chance to watch her work.

She'd have the prosecution tied in knots and the judge in the palm of her hand.

Claire took a seat that faced the door. As she reviewed her notes, she watched for Chris. Every time the door opened, she glanced up, and was disappointed each time it wasn't him.

She drank another cup of coffee and waited, doodling idly on the edges of the yellow pad.

Christopher Ryan Gabriel, she wrote, before scratching out the evidence of the ridiculous schoolgirl inside her that felt giddy just saying his name.

When, at last, he stepped through the door, resplendent in his dress blues, she nearly burst with delight. He was the picture of spit and polish, with rows of ribbons bespeaking his accomplishments. Even the dark shadows beneath his eyes were not as noticeable. He didn't look just good, he looked dazzling.

She watched him speak with the hostess, giving her the sweet, oh-so-polite smile, and then he looked her way. When he smiled at her across the crowded restaurant, Claire could barely breathe.

Over breakfast, she pulled herself from silliness and tried to have a professional conversation with her client.

"Do you trust me to defend you, Chris?"

He paused before answering, making her wonder for a moment.

"Implicitly."

Her heart soared with his confidence.

"Will you take the stand in your own defense?"

"If I have to."

The waitress stopped by with a fresh Pepsi for Chris and checked the coffee pot.

"We need to have Detective Medina find Suzanne—"

"Claire, we don't need Suzanne."

"What if she killed him, Chris? We have to find her."

He looked away, pained.

"I know. It's just..."

"What if I can arrange with Medina to let you go in to get her once they locate her?"

He reached for her hand, covering it with his much larger one.

"Thanks, but...just be sure they handle her with care, okay? I can't do it. And, Claire, I'd prefer to not drag her through the mud in court, if we can help it."

"I'll tell him."

At her car, he smiled down at her, pulling her hand to his lips.

"I'll see you soon."

"You want to ride with me?"

"No, I need to make a stop on the way. I owe the lieutenant an apology."

She smiled and nodded. He truly was an honorable man.

He opened her door for her, and before closing it, crouched down.

"Claire?" His voice was suddenly small.

"Yeah, Champ?"

He looked away, hesitant.

"What is it, Chris?"

"Nothing," he said, shaking his head. "Claire?"

"Yes?" She reached out for him, concerned at his sudden uncertainty.

"Thank you," he said, finally bringing up his eyes to meet hers. "For everything."

"For everything?"

"For everything. Mostly, for believing in me. Thank you." His voice hitched.

"You're welcome."

He shut her door, and she pulled away from him and out onto the street, wishing this whole thing were over and done.

The prosecutor, Alan Fry, wasn't just cocky. He was cocky in a greasy, slimy way that gave you the creeps. Claire hated cocky. Confident was one thing. Cocky—something else. But she could use that to her advantage.

Brumby was busy gathering the correct information to subpoena the desk clerk at the Lazy 8. He'd fax her the additional pages she'd need to provide to both the court and the prosecution. Maybe she'd have the opportunity to push for dropping the charges altogether.

The courtroom door opened, and she turned, expecting to see Chris. She smiled when she saw Cruz. He was in dress blues as well, present to give his friend support. He was quickly followed by the lieutenant, who nodded to her, then took a seat in the back row.

At ten 'til nine, there was no sign of her client.

At five 'til nine, she stepped back as nonchalantly as possible to sit beside Lt. Quillen.

"Where's your client, Captain?" he asked tersely.

"Last I knew he was headed to see you."

He shook his head.

She looked past the lieutenant to Cruz, who shrugged, then made her way out to the hall. When his voicemail picked up, she left a message she was sure sounded frantic.

The Honorable Judge Robert Short entered the room at nine-oh-three.

By nine ten, Claire's request for ten minutes ticked away, and she was struggling to catch her breath.

Fry was gloating.

At nine fifteen, the judge issued a bench warrant, and with the clap of his gavel, dismissed any further discussion.

Chapter Nineteen

Claire stood at attention as the judge left the bench. When she turned, the lieutenant was already gone, and Cruz fixed her with a glare before making his escape.

Grabbing her papers and her attaché case, she sprinted from the courthouse, catching Quillen before he pulled his Air Force sedan out into traffic.

"He didn't come by to see you, Lieutenant?"

"No, Captain, he didn't."

"Do you know where he might be?"

"Not a clue."

"Bastard," she hissed to no one in particular.

Cruz thought he might puke. Then, he thought he might not puke. Even when Gabe had sent him the deed to his building, it had never really occurred to him that Gabe might jump bail, that his plane and car would be forfeit.

"Holy Mary, mother of God," he muttered, thinking instantly of the red head that used that phrase in a most un-Catholic way when she was at a loss for words.

He liked that car.

He loved that plane.

Loved.

Past tense.

He owned the note on Kit's Jet Ranger, but it was no substitute. It was like buying a new puppy when the family dog was not yet cold in the ground. Sure the new dog might be fun. Eventually. But it didn't fill the gaping hole.

"Friggin' Gabriel," he said, slamming his car door.

When the rest of the team looked up, surprised to see him this soon, he waved them off. "Don't friggin' ask."

First Cruz came in, still in his Class A's. He was closely followed by the lieutenant, still in his. They also wore matching expressions that Will could only guess meant things at the courthouse had gone from worse to worser.

When Captain Janova came in fifteen minutes later, she looked like she'd lost her best friend. She also looked mighty pissed about it. In his official capacity as knower of all things worth knowing, Will forced himself to wander into the hallway to listen.

"Cruz, my office."

Three very unhappy but well-dressed personnel assembled quickly and closed the door behind them.

"I'm sorry, Lieutenant," Claire said, not knowing what else to say. Her ass was in a sling, and as much as that hurt, she'd let Quillen go out on the limb as well.

He looked at her, opened his mouth to reply, then shut it again and sat down.

Minutes ticked by. The only sound in the room was him drumming his fingers on his desk.

"Find him, Cruz," he said at last, not looking up. "You...effing...find him."

Then he looked up, his face flushed.

"Beg your pardon, ma'am."

Cruz started pacing, as much as one could pace in the small office.

"Sir, with all due respect, I'm not sure I'm the one who should find him."

No one would say his name. Claire wasn't sure what that meant, but found it mildly interesting.

"Go on."

"If I find him, sir, I might kill him."

For an instant, Claire didn't doubt the veracity of the words. He looked like he could inflict serious harm at the moment.

"I'm sorry about your plane, Cruz. You have sixty days..." She shut up when he shot her a look of pure rage.

Without another word, Cruz pivoted and left the room, closing the door behind him.

Now, the lieutenant smiled briefly, before shaking his head.

"Dismissed, I guess."

Then he looked at Claire.

"What was the *sixty-days* thing?"

"If someone jumps bond, the guarantor has sixty days to help find him before actually losing his surety."

"Oh, well, that's good, I suppose. What now, Captain?"

"Now, David," she wasn't sure where that came from but at this point, didn't much care, "I guess I tuck my tail between my legs and throw myself on my commander's mercy. You?"

"I don't know, but I'm not much looking forward to the conversation."

"No kidding."

On her way out to the car, she passed by the redhead that Cruz had taken to the party on Saturday. Her stride and expression had Claire idly wondering how much worse Cruz's day was about to get.

It took Eric about two minutes to shed the blues and throw on his flight suit. Even if he tried to find Gabriel, where would he start?

Watching credit cards took time.

He grabbed his phone and dialed.

"You friggin' liar," he told the voicemail, "you better friggin' call me."

Okay, first things first.

He'd get the current value of Gabriel's building—if this thing went further to hell, he was not going to lose his plane. Maybe he could swap the paper on the building for the paper on the plane and the Jeep.

He grabbed the phone again.

"You friggin' owe me rent, you lying dirt bag. And if you don't call me, I'm claiming all your earthly possessions."

Then, he'd get on the laptop and start seeing what he could find.

He headed toward the front door.

Kit's perfume.

He should have ducked.

She connected with a *thwack* that would have done Maureen O'Hara proud. As a matter of fact, at the moment she looked a bit like the fiery redhead that kept John Wayne on his toes. Beautiful and all blustery with rage.

Rubbing his cheek, he couldn't help but be both impressed and maybe a bit enchanted.

"Mary Katherine Sheridan."

"Don't."

The hand she put up to stop him shook, and she was clearly winding up to let him have it again.

Will and Matt had come from the dayroom.

Kit stepped up close, right in his face.

"Did you consider telling me that you'd screwed me over before kissing me, Cruz?"

She glanced over her shoulder at the guys and then turned back to Cruz.

"You may own my helicopter, and by extension, I suppose, my business. But if you think you own me, you've got another think coming."

She turned to leave and made it about ten yards before stopping and slowly coming about.

"And how does it feel, Hollywood, to lose your aircraft," she snapped her fingers, "just like that?"

She smirked, slowly turned, and walked out.

Now he was pretty sure he'd puke.

By eleven o'clock, Claire had done five hundred meters. Hard, fast, as if she could outrun the truth.

Chris had fled.

It wasn't just court he'd run out on. It was her. Is that what he'd been trying to tell her at the car earlier? That he wouldn't be there. That he was jumping bond?

Thanking her for everything?

For believing him? For defending him? For letting him get away?

God, what a fool she'd been.

What a fool she still was.

She swam harder, faster, pushing away the water, trying to push away everything else.

It didn't matter if he was innocent or not.

At a thousand meters, she stopped at the deep end and tried to catch her breath. It wasn't swimming that stole it. She pushed on.

And on.

She'd call Grisham and tell him what had happened. Request leave to come home. Be on a plane by this afternoon.

Forget California.

Forget being so completely taken in.

Forget Christopher Ryan Gabriel.

And if they ever caught up with him, he'd need a good lawyer. And that lawyer would not be her.

Could not be her.

Because, despite the resolve, she couldn't ever forget.

At fifteen hundred meters, she stopped, gulping in air as if she were drowning. Then, ignoring all propriety, she folded her arms on the edge, laid her head on them, and sobbed.

The call to Grisham was pure hell. Not because he ranted or railed, but more because he didn't. His disappointment was crystal clear.

Sometimes things just went to hell and there was nothing to be done.

Of course, she had leave to come home.

He'd save her the call and tell Airman Brumbelow to get her a flight back as soon as possible. Details would follow.

That left only packing, which would take minutes. It was the hours that she dreaded.

Will stood in the doorway to the dayroom.

Gabe hadn't shown up for court and the judge issued a warrant for his arrest. Sucked for the lieutenant, who had assured Gabe's continued presence. Sucked even more for Cruz.

And Cruz's diabolical plan had sort of fallen apart as well, unless he'd actually intended for Sheridan to hate him. If that was his intention, it had worked like a charm.

But, why would Gabe not show up?

Cruz was closeted back in one of the cubicles they used for report writing. Or at least that's what the cubicles were supposed to be used for. The guys wrote most reports from one of the La-Z-Boys and used the cubicles for naps.

Will risked stepping back there.

"Cruz?"

"What?" Cruz shouted.

"I thought I'd see if you needed any help."

No doubt he was playing bounty hunter at the moment.

"No."

And in no mood for civilities, either.

"Hey, Eric?"

"What, Clancy?"

"I can't see Gabe missing court of his own free will. I mean if he ran, then none of us knew him at all."

Cruz's eyebrows drew together, and he stared at Will as if his words had been jumbled.

Then, he closed his eyes. "Damn it."

Will waited for the thoughts to process. This wasn't rocket science.

Cruz jumped to his feet and dashed past, snagging Will's uniform and dragging him to the lieutenant's office.

"Tell him," Cruz ordered.

"What?"

"Tell Yoda what you just said to me."

Okay, Cruz was seriously losing it. Perhaps it was coup-contrecoup from Red's slap.

"I just said..."

But Cruz didn't let him finish.

"I was just so pissed, sir, I didn't even consider that he might not have had a choice. Jesus Christ, sir. Permission to go find him, sir."

Then spinning around, Cruz flew from the room, leaving Will and Yoda staring at his wake.

The lieutenant snapped his fingers quickly, his usual signal for "keep up, boys."

"Already had him working on that, sir?"

DQ shook his head dumbly. "You got it."

Back in the cubicle, Will ventured to speak again, but not without serious doubts on the wisdom of doing so.

"What if he got a phone call, Cruz?"

"On it," Cruz replied, tapping away furiously on the keyboard. He stopped long enough to throw a yellow pad at Clancy. "Make your skills useful, and list every possibility. Then, we'll work through them 'til we find him."

"I just hope..."

"Don't say it, Clance."

Chris sat in his car, trying to figure out what to do next. The Hyatt had thirty rooms on each of three floors. He was pretty sure she was on three, but there was no guarantee.

He should call Cruz.

Cruz would know what to do. He could hack the hotel computer and find her.

Under what name?

He'd tried every name he could think she might use.

Cruz was good at that stuff. Not only because of his intelligence experience, but also because he thought like a criminal. Well, at least more than Gabe did.

Not that Suz was a criminal. She still might be a victim.

And she was at the courthouse why?

To clear him?

Maybe it wasn't her, after all. And he threw away his career and Cruz's plane for nothing.

Of course, it was her. She took off when he saw her. And he'd had trouble following her here. Kind of surprised he'd been able to.

He'd gotten to the elevator just in time to see it stop on the third floor. She could have gotten off before three and made the elevator go up there to throw him off. He was pretty sure she didn't see him, though. So, third floor.

He needed Cruz.

No doubt Cruz would not welcome the phone call.

Maybe he could do this himself and call Cruz once he'd found out what room she was in.

From across the lot, he kept his gaze fixed on her car. She couldn't leave without it.

Claire's phone startled her. She'd been intently reading the ticker on the bottom of the Fox News channel, trying hard to not go completely stir crazy. She didn't wait well.

"Janova," she barked.

"You don't need to bite my head off."

"Sorry, Brian."

Brumby read her the itinerary, and she jotted down flights and times. He'd gotten lucky, finding a flight out of Merced instead of Fresno that left in an hour and a half. She could leave right now, drop her rental at a full sprint, and make it through TSA with no time to think.

Perfect.

Chapter Twenty

When he saw the airport shuttle pull up to the front doors, Chris realized he'd been wrong.

Suz *could* leave without her car.

Damn it all.

An idea, if you could call it that, sparked to life in his muddled brain.

Cringing, he reached for the key and started the 'Vette. He did the only thing he could think of to do.

He rammed the 'Vette into the back of her car.

Then, he put on his jacket, buttoned it up, and headed back to the front desk.

He waited until the clerk he'd spoken to before wandered away, then he went in for the kill, wishing he could summon charm the way Cruz could.

"Excuse me, ma'am," he said to the new girl, "I had an accident with a car in your parking lot. Here's the license plate number," he said, handing her the scrap of paper. "I need to exchange insurance information with the owner, if you could give me the name and room number."

She started to help, then reconsidered.

Damn.

"Show me, sir."

He led her out to the parking lot where he'd left the 'Vette up against her car.

She cringed at the sight. "Oh, your poor 'Vette."

"Yeah," he said, not having to pretend.

"C'mon, let's see what we can find."

Cruz would say *cool*.

"Good."

"Cruz," Eric answered, distracted. Still typing.
"It's me."
"Gabe? Where are you? You okay?"
"I'm at the Hyatt. I'm fine."
"Jerk."
"Suz is here. I found her. Room three twenty-two."
Gabe sounded a little bit tickled by that information.
"I'll be right there."
"I'm going up to talk to her."
"Jesus, Gabe. She may be armed."

"She won't hurt me, Eric." He didn't sound sure. Sounded like he was reconsidering the statement. "I'll call you back. Let Claire know I didn't run out on her."

The line went dead.

"Moron," Cruz said, and he pushed to his feet, knocking the chair over on the way up.

Will flattened himself against the wall to keep from being run down as Cruz sprinted from the building. It was like a bad silent movie when he had to do it again after Cruz came back in at a full run, skidding to a halt at the office door.

"He's found her, sir. I tried to get him to wait until I got there to go in, but he's being stupid. They're at the Hyatt Hotel—room three twenty-two."

He paused.

"She's got a gun, sir."
"Got it. Go. I'll call the detective."

Chris knocked on the door.
"Yes?"
Good, she was still there.
"Room service," he said, then elaborated off of the cuff. "I have your mimosa."

He glanced at his watch. Way past mimosa time.
Too late. Damage done.
But the door opened.
And he had a clear-cut coulda-had-a-V8 moment when he looked in to see Suz holding a gun.
"Come in, Chris."

Nothing to be done but humor the one holding all the cards. He went in.

Not your ordinary hotel room. He wondered vaguely where the money came from for a suite like this.

"You told Max where I was."

"I'm sorry," he said, trying to figure out how to diffuse the situation. "Can I sit down?"

He'd learned a long time ago to get lower than a patient when you needed his cooperation. Something about towering over a person—which at his height was hard to avoid—put them on the defensive.

"Whatever."

"What happened, Suz?"

"When?" She walked to the window and looked out.

Cruz, please just stay put.

"When Max died."

"I shot him."

The way she said it turned him cold and any hope of this ending well went right out the door.

"Why?"

"Because he wanted to have me committed. You know he set me up in Iraq. I think he was working for al-Qaeda."

"What?"

"Yeah, we were both there, working on a case. He was prosecuting, I was defending. He went outside to get something from the car and the building came under mortar fire. I think he called it in. He wanted me out of the way."

Okay, the girl was seriously whacked.

"His parents might be sleepers, Gabe."

"Suz..."

Her eyes flashed, and she rushed at him, waving the gun in his face.

"Don't *Suz* me, Gabe. I'm not crazy. The doctor said so. But Max kept trying. He had them put me away for two weeks, and he wanted to do it again."

Gabe closed his eyes and waited for her to kill him.

He should have listened to Cruz.

But that would mean Cruz would be here beside him, getting shot as well.

He wished he could see Claire, explain. Tell her...

169

"Gabe."

He opened his eyes.

"Why'd you tell him? You promised."

Her eyes filled with tears, and he thought for a minute that she was going to put down the gun. But then she turned back to the window.

"I'm sorry," he said.

Maybe he could tackle her.

She was about six feet away.

"It was an accident. I didn't mean to kill him. I just wanted him to leave me alone."

As unobtrusively as he could, Chris inched forward on his chair.

"He kept babbling about me taking his money and coming toward me. I just wanted him to leave."

What was she talking about?

"What money?" he asked before he could stop himself.

She fluttered her free hand in the air and shook her head quickly.

"The money in the duffle bags. Three of them."

When she jumped back into the story, he didn't interrupt again.

"He walked forward. Kept saying I wouldn't shoot him. Kept coming until the gun was right against his chest."

She took in a ragged breath.

Maybe he could get her to put down the gun.

"Then he yelled at me, screamed something, scared me. The gun went off..."

A knock at the door drew her attention.

And her aim.

Cruz.

Before Chris could get her down, knocking her back, she fired at the door.

Glass shattered. She hit the coffee table.

The gun fell. Chris grabbed it. Then he charged for the door, yanking it open.

"Cruz!"

Eric lay on the floor, panting.

"I'm okay, but Jesus, Gabe."

Gabe turned back to Suz, and his gut twisted.

By the time Cruz got to his feet and into the room, Gabe was covered with blood.

He sat on the floor, rocking Suzanne in his arms, begging her not to die.

But it was seriously too late. They both knew it.

The coffee table lay in shattered shards, one of which had killed her.

She'd bled out almost instantly.

But Gabe still held her. Still rocking.

Chapter Twenty One

Claire stood at the window and looked out at the nose of the plane that waited to take her home.

They'd already called the first-class passengers to load.

She swallowed the lump in her throat and reached for her phone when it rang.

"Captain Janova."

"Claire, where are you?" Cruz.

"At the airport."

"You need to come to the Hyatt Hotel in Merced."

"Cruz, I'm done."

"Suzanne is dead."

"And Chris?" she asked. She kicked herself for doing so.

"Needs you."

"Me, or an attorney."

"Both. Come to room three twenty-two. The police are on their way, so hurry."

"Did he kill her, Cruz?"

"In a manner of speaking. Are you coming?"

"Yeah, I'll be right there."

She grabbed her attaché and raced for the exit.

Claire arrived right behind Medina. He waited for the elevator. She sprinted up the stairs, getting to the room out of breath, but before Medina.

What she saw when she entered the room left her shaky, to say the least.

She took a deep breath and braced herself.

"I'd have covered her up, but it's a crime scene, so I left her," Cruz said, looking over from where he stood by the window.

Chris sat in the chair a few feet away, head down, twisting his Academy ring on bloody hands.

When he looked up at her, she realized he was covered in blood.

The look in his eyes, though, was what ripped her heart out.

She stilled herself, not wanting to run from the room. Not wanting to run to him.

She'd seen the look on his face before, but not like now.

Tortured.

"What happened?" She asked.

"That's what I'd like to know."

Medina.

She whirled around.

"Not this time, bubba," she said striding toward him. "Eric, please keep Detective Medina company out in the hall. I will have a word with my client. And Eric, don't say a word."

"Yes, ma'am," he said, smiling. Then he turned to the cop and shrugged. "Orders."

She turned again to Medina. "So you can be assured of the sanctity of the crime scene, I'll leave the door open. But my conversation with my client is not yours to hear."

Throwing all the rules to the wind, she walked slowly over to Chris and laid her hand on his head, taking a moment to just touch his hair. Then she lowered herself to the floor at his feet and waited for him to speak.

Cruz had to give the guy credit.

"Your lieutenant called me and sent me here, Sergeant Cruz. I think you can tell me what happened. He said Sergeant Gabriel was here, trying to get Max's wife to surrender."

Cruz just looked at him and smiled.

He doubted those were DQ's exact words.

"You know, I can take you into custody and sort it out later."

"My attorney's inside," Cruz replied, nodding his head toward the half-closed door.

The closed door with a bullet hole in it.

Glancing across at the corresponding hole in the wall, he thanked the powers that be that. Plane or no plane, car or no car, Red or no Red, the bullet had missed him.

He stepped closer, stood with his back against the wall, estimating, cringing at where the bullet would have hit if he'd not watched way too much TV and actually been standing there.

Cold dread raced down his back.

He might not get to ever kiss Red again, but at least he lived to love again.

The door opened, and Claire stepped out.

"You can come in, Jim. Eric, do you mind waiting?"

"I'm good. Everything okay in there?"

She shrugged as Medina stepped past her.

"I think so. He's pretty distraught, but I think I've got it under control."

"Thanks for coming, Claire."

"I didn't have much choice."

"Because you're a good attorney?"

"Yeah, right. Because I'm a good attorney."

He smiled at her. She smiled back. Or tried to.

"When this is all over, Claire..."

She waved him off. "Can't think about that right now, Eric."

"Right."

After running through the ground rules—the detective would sit and listen to her client's story and he would say nothing until her client was finished, then *she* would field any questions he had—she leaned over to Chris, and laid her hand on his shoulder.

"You can tell him what you told me, Chris."

His gaze met hers, and she nodded her encouragement.

"It's okay. Take your time. I won't let you fall."

"Everything?"

"Yeah, Chris. Everything."

She looked up to Medina, and for the first time since the day they met, she saw a man who was no longer an adversary. He gave her a small smile and nodded.

Chris started slowly, talking in his usual soft voice. Soon, he seemed to gather strength, sat up straight, and finished the story.

"My car is down there, smashed into her rental. It's rented to Virginia Washington."

He shook his head, then looked over at Claire and smiled.

"Virginia Washington. Some alias, huh?" Then back to Medina, "She used the same one here. Paid cash, presumably from the stash she found. She didn't say where."

"Do you know where this stash of money is now, Sergeant?"

"No."

"Strange as it seems, I actually believe you, Sergeant." He turned to Claire, "Keep your client nearby, Captain, until we can process the scene and the car. We'll be in touch."

When Chris didn't get up, Medina reminded him that he was free to go. Chris stood then, and putting his hand on the small of Claire's back, ushered her out.

At the door, she turned.

"Jim, would you be so kind as to call the DA? Let him know why Chris wasn't in court. Maybe start the process of getting the bench warrant cleared. I'll go down there shortly and see if I can get the bond money released."

"Yeah, I will," he said, turning away, toward the body.

The Coroner waited in the hall.

Claire seemed distant, standing a few feet away in the elevator, walking out to his car. She was quiet.

The insurance agent, who Cruz had called for him, stood with the uniformed officer looking at the damage to the 'Vette. His baby was pretty seriously crunched. Fiberglass. But all in all, it was worth it. He could probably still drive it.

"Where's your car?" he asked Claire, turning to glance through the lot.

"I took a taxi."

"Oh."

Claire looked away, then turned slowly toward him, not bringing her eyes up to his. It was the first that he'd noticed. She wasn't in uniform. She was wearing jeans.

"Where were you when Cruz called?" He ground the words out.

"At the airport."

"Oh."

She looked up, biting her lip. The first time he'd seen uncertainty on her face. She shrugged. "I'm sorry."

What did he expect? That, even in the face of his disappearance, she'd stand by him? Even though he'd left her hanging?

"No, Claire, I'm sorry. You have no need to apologize. Thank you for coming back. For taking care of all this."

The insurance guy approached. Chris nodded politely and listened to the guy babble on about estimates and loaner cars. When he moved on to how his first car had been a Corvair back in the '60's, Chris intervened, thanking the guy and telling him he'd be in touch. Then he turned back to Claire.

"You need a ride to the airport?"

"No. I, uh, need to go by the courthouse. Get all the paperwork cleared. Try to get Cruz's money back."

"I signed over my building to him."

He wasn't at all sure why he'd told her that. But it made her smile.

"Of course, you did."

"A ride to the courthouse then?"

"Nah, I'll grab a cab. I'll let you know how it goes."

"Okay."

She turned and walked back inside. He wished he could say something to get...what?

"Can you drive her?" Cruz asked, coming up behind him, taking in the sad sight before him.

"Yeah, I can."

Cruz slapped him on the back.

"You want a beer?"

"Yeah, I do."

"It's not five o'clock yet, boys." DQ approached from the lobby.

They turned in unison.

"Apparently, I missed all the excitement, huh? Captain Janova gave me the abbreviated version."

"Yes, sir, you did," Cruz said, wearing his I-saved-the-world-single-handedly grin. "But Gabe here did us proud..."

Cruz looked at Chris, then stopped.

"Sorry, man."

Gabe nodded. "It's okay. Sir, join us for a beer?"

"As they say, it's five o'clock somewhere. I need to speak with the colonel, and you need to shower and change. I'll meet you at the Oasis in an hour."

Claire caught the judge as he was leaving. He was in a hurry to pick up his kids from daycare, but said he'd do his best to get the bond money released.

"We don't have this kind of thing happen around here, Captain. At least not for a very long time."

"No doubt. Merced seems like a nice town."

"It is. I'll do my best for you. Come by in the morning—say, eight thirty? Now, I really need to get outta here."

"Thanks."

Claire walked out with him, then sat down on the steps to the courthouse. The afternoon sun was warm, but fall was definitely in the air. The light was diffused, almost sad.

Or maybe that was just her, projecting her feelings onto the universe.

With a deep sigh, she pulled out her phone and called in.

"I don't know what to say, sir, but I'm still in Merced. My bags are on the plane, but I'm not."

"Do tell, Captain."

Her rank came out stiffly. His patience was clearly at its end. She could hardly blame him for that.

It took her a few minutes to fill him in on the happenings of the afternoon.

"Your client is alive and well."

"Well, he's pretty shook, sir."

"And two of my JAGS are dead. Captain..."

Claire waited, wishing she had the words that would make everything okay.

"Call me tomorrow, I guess, Claire. I'll have someone pick up your things on this end."

"Yes, sir. Thank you, sir."

"Good night, Captain."

"Night, sir."

She tucked the phone into her bag and started to push to her feet. Instead, she just sat, closed her eyes, and breathed in the cool air.

How had her life spun so suddenly out of her control? Since this whole thing started, she'd done little right. She'd broken most of the rules in her office, and she'd broken important rules of ethics.

She'd put her poor commander through a roller coaster of on-again-off-again lawyering. Granted, some of that was not her doing.

Most of all, she'd let it all get so personal that now, sitting here in the late California sun, she couldn't figure out how to untangle her heart from the thorns that held her fast. At last, she stood and started walking, thinking that maybe she could find a bite to eat.

A few blocks later, she found herself standing across the street from Chris's place, looking up at the windows, which only reflected the blue of the sky. She took two more steps toward the street, then stopped.

The last time she felt so jumbled was probably high school. It was that odd thing where you longed to see him, yet terrified you would. While it was uncomfortable, feeling silly and jittery and nearly sick with it, it was also warm and wonderful.

That's when he pulled into the parking space down the block. He didn't see her. He looked tired and forlorn carrying his bloody blues jacket over his shoulder. Despite all that, he was so very handsome.

She watched him disappear through the door and looked up, hoping he'd reappear at the window.

When he didn't, she turned away.

But five steps later, she changed her mind.

And her direction.

Chris unbuttoned his shirt and tossed it into the trash can. He might be able to salvage the slacks but the jacket—

he doubted that even the best dry cleaner could get all the blood out. He wasn't sure he wanted them to try.

His jacket? Really? He was worried about his damn jacket?

He'd put his career on the line. His life on the line. For what? Both Max and Suzanne were dead.

And even though he knew in his head that he wasn't responsible...

He squeezed his eyes shut.

"Why..."

He heard the door slide open, and he walked out. Hoping.

When he saw her there, standing in the doorway, something in him broke loose. Like a log jam.

As he got close, she put her bag on the floor.

Tears streamed down her beautiful face.

Neither of them spoke as he pulled her into his arms.

It might have been simple exhaustion, or maybe just relief, but the emotions of the past week ganged up on him, and he cried.

They stood, holding on for dear life, until the storm passed and they were able to breathe again.

"That was Gabe," Cruz said. "He's not going to make it."

"He okay?" Will asked.

Everyone who'd been at the Section when DQ came back wanted to hear the details. The lieutenant told them that Cruz and Gabe were headed to the Oasis—as soon as Gabe changed out of his bloody clothes. That upped their attention significantly. Now, they all sat at one big table, waiting for the story.

"Yeah, he's fine. Claire's there."

One of the Alpha guys made a suggestive sound, earning him angry scowls all around.

"They're pretty good together," Cowboy said.

At Will's look, Cowboy shrugged.

"Don'cha think?"

"Yeah, actually, I do. I just didn't think you'd notice."

"Hello. I'm not blind. I might not be the sharpest crayon in the box. But hello."

When that drew a smile, Cowboy was off and running, letting loose all the humor he'd had corralled for days. Either he was really funny, which he was, or they were all very relieved, which they were.

The reality was that none of them had wanted to think the Angel Gabriel guilty, but none of them could quite get themselves to discount the evidence, either.

Now, they could let down their guards.

"What's the word of the day, Clancy?" DQ asked.

"Manumission," he replied, then took a drink.

At their dumb looks, he raised his glass.

"It means freedom from slavery or bondage. Cheers."

While Chris showered, Claire ordered pizza and poured wine. Then, with less than enthusiasm, she called and reserved a room at the Best Western.

"You could have stayed here."

"I know."

She was nervous and awkward suddenly.

He drew up behind her at the window, laying his hands on her shoulders. He didn't speak. Maybe he was just as tongue-tied as she was.

The pizza came. They sat on the couch and ate. They drank wine while soft jazz played on the stereo.

But they still didn't talk.

As time passed, though, the silence became less awkward, more companionable. Cozy. Nice.

"Would you have stayed here with me tonight if Suz hadn't slept in my bed?"

"Oh." She hadn't even considered that. "I don't know."

Another long silence.

"Were you able to get Cruz's money back?"

"I caught the judge on his way out. He promised he'd take care of it first thing in the morning."

He nodded, then laid his head back and closed his eyes.

"What then, Claire?"

"Grisham wants me back."

"Was there any doubt? You're a great lawyer. When do you have to leave?"

"Probably tomorrow."

He sat up and turned to her, taking her hands.

She thought he was going to ask her to stay, but he didn't.

She thought he was going to kiss her, but he didn't.

At last, he brought her hands to his lips, holding them there, looking at her.

Then he stood and walked to the window.

"You want to take the car?"

The absence of his asking if he could drive her to the motel was glaring.

"No, I'll call a cab."

Chapter Twenty Two

The phone on the bedside table rang, jarring her, even though she wasn't asleep.

The clock said twelve-oh-two.

She smiled and picked up.

"You should be asleep," she said.

"I love you, Claire."

"I love you, too, Chris."

"But that doesn't really change anything, does it?' Chris asked.

"I don't know."

"You fill a void inside me that I didn't even know I had."

Now was not the time. The stress from the past week, the relief of having it over. No good decisions could be made now.

"Chris..."

"Night, Claire."

"Night."

Chris went in to work. He didn't know what else to do. At first, he felt that same strange awkwardness. But as soon as he stepped into the locker room and a bucket of water dropped on his head, he was home.

Alpha team was called out early to assist on a mission in Utah, leaving Bravo with the weekly to-do list. Cruz reminded anyone who would listen how wrong that was on every level.

At ten, Cruz's phone rang. It was Claire.

"She said the judge was called out of town late last night, and he'd be back tomorrow afternoon. She has a three o'clock appointment with him."

"I'm sorry, Cruz."

"Don't worry about it, pal. It'll all work out."

"God, I hope so."

Claire didn't call him, though. Maybe he'd dreamed her words last night. Or maybe, loving someone wasn't enough. In what he knew was an insane action, he picked up the phone and dialed.

He got her voicemail.

"Cruz says you'll be here through tomorrow. Since you'll be here anyway, want to watch me give away the bride?"

"You're pathetic," Cruz said from the hallway.

"No doubt."

"It just occurred to me that you need new blues for tomorrow night. It wouldn't do at all for you to look better than the rest of us."

"Right."

The closest Base Exchange, where you could actually buy blues off the rack was at Travis. Too far. Chris had not ever been able to actually buy off the rack. He wasn't as stocky as most guys his height. He could order a set from here but it would take too long to get here.

"C'mon, let's go see if my other set can be emergency tailored. If not, we'll raid Nic's closet." Cruz said.

Chris let Cruz take control—like he really had any choice. But it seemed to make Cruz happy, so what the hell.

"You think she'll come?" Eric asked on the way to his place.

Chris could only shrug.

"Don't let her get away, dude."

He laughed, "Said the expert in the field of love. Will told me about your—um—visit from the queen."

"Of course, he did. The only thing that boy ever kept to himself was your secret. You'd have been proud."

"You're avoiding the topic, Hollywood."

"Damn right, I am."

At three o'clock on Wednesday afternoon, good to his word, Judge Short took a recess and saw Claire in his office. He handed her the paperwork and informed her that Sergeant Cruz could arrange to pick up his bond any time. That left only a twenty-thousand-dollar hole in Cruz's pocket.

"We don't do this under normal circumstances, Captain."

He was very serious, and she refrained from reminding him that there was nothing normal about the circumstances and that, under California law, they were obligated to return the bond if the bad guy was found right away. Instead, she shook his hand and thanked him profusely. In retrospect, sucking up seemed an okay thing to do for one hundred eighty thousand dollars, even if it wasn't hers.

When she was finished, she went back to her room and watched the clock. She had every intention of letting this thing cool off for a while, so both she and Chris could look at it again in the light of normal day. She had no intention of going to a wedding. Way too dangerous.

And yet, at a quarter 'til six, there she was, sitting in the back of the Club, waiting to see Julie and her champion walk down the makeshift aisle.

Chris glanced again at his watch. It was six straight up, and the bride was still sequestered in the back room. With a whole lot of trepidation, he wandered that way and knocked timidly at the door.

Julie's friend came to the door, her eyes wide with concern.

"Everything okay?" Gabe whispered.

She tipped her hand back and forth indicating that things could be better.

"Tell you what. You stand guard, and I'll see if I can help."

The girl shrugged.

Julie sat gazing out the window at the fading light. She wore a satiny robe. If she heard him come in, she didn't let on.

He joined her on the bench.

"Hi, sweetheart,"

Her gaze shifted to his.

"You okay?"

She only nodded.

"Missing your family?"

Again, she nodded, then shook her head. She held up her hand and took a deep breath.

"I don't know if I'm strong enough."

"For what, babe?"

"To let him go."

He slipped his arm around her. She felt so small against him.

He knew exactly what she meant. Since the moment Nic had broken the news, Chris carried a dread deep inside.

"None of us is strong enough, Julie. At least not on our own. There aren't any guarantees here and I know that terrifies you."

She trembled against him now.

If he could have promised her Nic would return to them untouched, he would have.

"We're all in this together, and we'll hang on to each other and deal with whatever comes."

For the next few minutes, he held her. Finally, she wiped her eyes and stood up.

"Nic will think I changed my mind. I'd better get dressed."

Chris leaned close and kissed the top of her head.

"Enjoy every moment, sweetie."

"Yeah. Thanks, Angel."

It was his turn to only nod.

The bride wore light blue, not white. Well, light blue with tiny pink and white flowers. She looked so pretty. Her blonde hair was down, just as Claire had always seen it, nothing special. The dress was a simple sundress with cap sleeves that showed how tan Julie was. She had on blue sandals. The only real concession was the beautiful bouquet she carried. Claire was able to identify the Tropicana roses, Shasta daisies, and was trying to figure out what the tiny burgundy flowers were when she made the mistake of looking up.

She'd seen Chris in Class A's only days before.

She hadn't seen *this* Chris in dress uniform. He was very serious, yet the tension had all but drained from his face. If anything, he stood taller, might have even gained a little weight.

He caught her eye without turning his head and gave her the slightest nod of acknowledgment. And then he was by her, walking Julie to the front, where her handsome groom stood.

Nic was very sober as he watched her approach.

Cruz was beside him and leaned over to whisper something. Nic smothered a smile and returned to solemn, but not quite so much.

Julie had only one attendant, so Cowboy and Clancy, wearing their Class A's as well, stood to the side. It was truly a team event. The lieutenant and the other PJs were spread out in the first two rows on either side. There were only a few others in attendance.

When they reached the front, Chris took Julie by the shoulders and leaned low to say something to her, then kissed her on the forehead.

Claire blinked away tears and told herself she never cried at weddings.

A chaplain performed the ceremony, which was short and sweet.

The mood was joyous with a thread of desperation and foreboding throughout.

The groom kissed the bride, and Claire thought they held on to each other a bit longer than she'd ever seen before.

They only had tonight and tomorrow.

Nic would fly out on Friday at noon.

Before she dissolved, Claire snuck through a side door.

The party moved out onto the back porch quickly enough. Chris had been surprised and pleased to see Claire as he walked Julie down the aisle. It had taken control to not stop and...

And what? Beg her to stay?

She couldn't stay.

He was certain the only reason she was still here had to be that she couldn't get a flight out until tomorrow.

Since she left his house the other night, he hadn't seen her. The midnight phone call was the last time he'd spoken with her. That conversation felt more like a dream than reality.

Yet, she'd been here. Someone had told her where and when. Not him.

Chris walked along the path to the gazebo. He stopped, leaning against the railing and looked out into the distant twilight. He might have been there minutes, or he might have been there hours.

But then, she was there beside him, laying her hand on his. He held his breath.

"Nice wedding, even if it was a bit melancholy," she said.

Sweet Jesus. Fear was a stone in his belly, sand in his mouth.

After a bit, Claire went on. "We've known each other for only days. Neither of us is the settle-down-and-have-kids type. We live across the country from each other. Any expert would tell us our chances were slim to none."

Hope sprung eternal.

The fear began to dissipate, replaced by the feeling you got when you stepped off a cliff into the dark. But he liked that feeling.

A lot.

He held onto his words.

"What do you want to do, Chris?"

He curled his fingers around hers, but didn't turn, didn't look over at her.

The answer that came to mind—what he really wanted—sounded insane. When he couldn't get his mouth to work, she stepped in again.

"I don't want to get two years down the road and wonder if we could have proved the experts wrong."

He chanced an answer.

"I want to take you to Paris and marry you under the Eiffel Tower."

He ventured a look in her direction.

She was smiling, squeezing his hand.

"For someone not into flowers and romance, that sounded pretty romantic."

He shrugged.

She laughed.

"Tell you what, Champ, two weeks from Friday, we all have a three-day weekend. I'll fly to Vegas and check into the Paris hotel. If you show up, we'll get married under the Eiffel Tower."

"Like *An Affair to Remember?*" he said.

She glanced over at him. "You saw that movie?"

"No, but I saw *Sleepless in Seattle*."

It was her turn to be struck dumb.

He turned and drew her to face him. She wouldn't look up, so he lifted her chin 'til her eyes met his. She was embarrassed, scared.

"I wouldn't miss it for the world."

She let out the breath she was holding and smiled. Then she tucked herself against his chest and put her arms around his waist.

"I love you, Christopher Ryan Gabriel."

"And I love you, despite my glaring ignorance of your middle name."

"That's okay, Sergeant. I won't hold that against you."

"Thank you, Captain."

"You want to go inside and drink champagne? Celebrate with your friends?"

"Yeah, as long as you'll come with me."

"I will."

Epilogue

From: Hollywood <hollywood1@pjmail.net>
To: Batman <batman@pjmail.net>
Subject: Angel and the Pretty Woman

Batman,

Got your email. Sounds like you're surviving the heat. We've had a real cooldown here, but I won't rub it in.

Chris and Claire got married on Saturday. We gave him a proper send-off and tipped a pint with your name on it. At one point, he was hoping his sisters could fly in. I assured him I'd show them the town. At that point, he changed his mind about getting them there. Was it something I said?

I flew him to Vegas and stood up for them. Claire said they'd come back every year and celebrate their anniversary by seeing another wonder of the world right there in Sin City. I wanted them to be married by an Elvis impersonator but they vetoed my vote. Rude.

They both had cold feet at the end. So I played Cupid—as I did with you and Julie—and asked them if they were better together than they were apart. They looked at each other and decided to go for it. My work there was done. Damn, I'm good.

I checked into the Hilton and lost too much money at the blackjack tables. All that was left was to hook up with a showgirl and get thrown out of the Star Trek experience. But that didn't work out, either. So I ended up alone in my room watching soccer.

Despite their separation, which Claire assures me is only temporary, I think they'll be fine. You and Julie will be, too.

I'd be fine if I could get laid.

Gotta go, I'm late for work.

Oh, forgot to tell you—there's a memo on the board saying that the crazy Aussie is coming. Guess he'll be here for a while working with Fraser over at SAR. It'll be good to see him. With all you old married folks around, things need a little shaking up.

Oh, and I start rotary wing flying lessons next weekend. Sheridan didn't offer to teach me, but even if she had, I wouldn't have taken her up on it. I think she'd have taken the first opportunity and tossed me out.

Julie's hanging in there, but she still refuses to move in with me. What's up with that?

We miss you, Batman.

Stay safe.

Hollywood

Look for Book Four in the *True Heroes* series...

TRUE VIRTUE

Don't bother running. You'll only die tired...

A former Navy SEAL who's afraid of sleeping in his own bed. How the mighty have fallen. When Daniel Fraser lost his wife to leukemia, he pretty much stopped living. He crawled into his cave and didn't come out. Now, his work, as Captain of the Yosemite Search and Rescue, is his sole raison d'être. Even sleep is something he rarely does, and when he does, it's on the couch.

Sophie Riene grew up pampered, to say the least, the daughter of a French CEO and a champion figure skater. Because she's an only child, her younger cousin Henri is more like a brother to her. They do everything together, including becoming top rated rock climbers. Together, they dream of the ultimate climb, El Capitan in Yosemite. But then, Henri loses his sight. So Sophie comes to Yosemite alone, determined to make her trip count for something. For Henri.

When Daniel is called in to rescue an injured climber, he smacks right into life again. In the person of a very adventurous Sophie Riene. Can Sophie get him to come out of his cave and live again? Even if she can, will he be able to save her when her life crumbles around her?

True Virtue is the fourth installment in the five-book True Heroes military romance series. If you love stories of finding love again, only to have darkness try to snatch it away, you'll find this book irresistible.

True Virtue Excerpt

PROLOGUE

Maybe it was the rain that seemed to have been coming down non-stop for weeks, making everything sloppy and everyone cranky. Whatever it was, McGee's bar was very quiet, even for a weeknight. Kevin Stabler, at the head of a table for eight, held court with a group of his co-workers. Rain was a major pain in the ass at construction sites. At least the building they'd been working on for the last month was under roof.

At the moment, the group was lamenting the closing of their favorite meeting place. The upcoming weekend was the last one for McGee's for the next two or three months. Renovation, the sign said.

"What about the Oasis?" one of the guys asked.

Kevin shook his head. That idea needed squashing right away. The 'O' was his "other" place and he didn't need any of these guys there.

"Nah, too many flyboy schmucks."

A group nod circled the table like the wave. None of Kevin's boys thought much of the Air Force Pararescue Jumpers - PJs for short. It was an opinion Kevin had carefully cultivated.

He kept the smile from reaching his lips. These guys were so easy.

"Hey guys," the newcomer said, laying a paper sack on the table and shrugging out of his wet coat.

"Jerry," Kevin nodded.

Jerry ordered another pitcher and grinned as he pulled a

magazine from the sack.

"I bring eye candy and good news for all of us."
Kevin watched as Jerry found the right spot in said magazine and passed it around.

"Meet Sophie Riene, boys."

Jerry allowed the group to have a look at the pictures and smiled smugly as the group groaned and drooled.

"Come to me, Sophie. On your knees, Sweetheart."

The magazine reached the end of the table and Kevin glanced at it in passing. He'd intended to pass it off again immediately, not interested in giving Jerry the satisfaction.

The road to hell is paved with good intentions.

He sucked in a breath through his teeth.

Holy shit.

Sophie Riene was something. The big picture showed Sophie standing boldly with hands on hips in a fancy, low-cut red dress that hugged every curve. She had dark hair--so long it tickled her perfect ass--and a delicate face. The smaller inset was a face shot that showed a sweet smile and brown-green eyes.

The text was in French and Kevin's French consisted of a few choice words that he learned on a trip to Baton Rouge as a teenager.

"Turn the page," Jerry said, his voice taking on a teasing tone.

Hoh-boy. Full page. Sophie in the flesh--wet flesh to boot--with only a fluffy towel hiding her most delicious parts.

Kevin cleared his throat and passed the magazine on. But the effect on his body was hard to ignore. It wasn't quite the effect that spending intimate time with Hustler gave him, but it was a start. Now Jerry piped up again.

"Sophie Riene is the daughter of the former CEO of Elf Aquitaine--it's one of the top ten oil and gas companies in the world. She's like the most eligible babe in all of France and guess what?" He waited for the desired response. Kevin worked to appear nonchalant.

"She's moved to Merced to spend time climbing and taking pictures in Yosemite. I'm thinking seriously about taking up climbing, myself."

His laugh was guttural--almost disgusting, even to Kevin ---and the group joined in.

God.

These guys were all talk. They wouldn't take up climbing. They wouldn't get any further than slobbering over pictures in a bar. If said French babe walked in here right now, even spread herself on the table for their pleasure, not one of these guys would even unzip. Not until he led the way.

Morons.

So, Frenchy was going to be hanging out in the park. Perfect. Kevin loved being in the right place at the right time. This time, he was unable to keep the smile from his face. Who knew when he joined SAR three months ago that he'd be putting himself in that very right place.

Score.

Kevin sat back down, sipping his beer, waiting for the flap to die down.

"You guys want me to scan the pictures and email them out to you?" he asked.

They heartily agreed and Jerry begrudged temporary custody of the magazine to Kevin.

The conversation soon changed and the decision was made, since Kevin didn't like the O, to move the party to the Alibi Lounge next week.

On his way home, Kevin swung by the SAR building intent on using the scanner there to grab the pictures. But, damned if the big boss Fraser wasn't there. At one-friggin'-o'clock in the morning. What an asshole.

CHAPTER ONE

As usual, Daniel Fraser couldn't sleep, even with the rain pattering on the windows. He'd stayed at the office past midnight, past maybe even one and yet here he sat.

On the couch.

Again.

And, as usual, he'd wake here in the morning.

Damn it.

If he could just bring himself to clean out the bedroom. Get all of Karen's presence out of there. He could even buy another bed.

Once again, he put it on his to-do list.

Even though he knew damn well he would ignore it.

Once again.

The couch was fine.

Especially when he spent most of his time, usually late into the night, at SAR HQ. Tonight--well, technically, last night--when Stan was headed out the door for the day, he'd turned to Daniel.

"You staying, Professor?"

"I'm leaving soon."

"At least say it like you mean it," Stan said, chuckling.

They both knew that he would be there late into the night.

New members, a new building--thank God--lots of work to do. It felt good, actually. Over the last week, he'd prepared a schedule for new training and he and the Board of Directors had worked on the open house coming up the first week of November.

It was nice building. Big. Even a climbing wall. And, at his insistence, there was a large den of sorts, complete with a kitchen, where the team could hang out. As long as he'd been here in Merced, he'd wanted the team to be closer, to spend time with each other in an informal setting.

SEALs formed close teams.

SAR could, too.

Sure, they'd all spent time at the Oasis after missions but he wanted more for the team. And now he had the place. Soon, he'd have the right furniture and a TV and stereo, maybe a pool table. The bonding part would be up to the members.

The team was bigger than when he'd left. Over the years, Stan had always argued for more members. During Daniel's two month sabbatical, Stan had taken advantage of his absence and had put on another dozen people, nine men and three women. Daniel didn't begrudge him. Stan had done a good job leading the team in Daniel's absence. Daniel hoped that his anal approach to filling team positions and Stan's much more casual approach--casual-- hell, he'd let anyone on the team--would not be cause for conflict.

Daniel pushed up from the couch and trudged to the kitchen, grabbing a bottle of water from the fridge before lowering himself to a kitchen chair. He pushed up his glasses, pressed his thumb and forefinger to the bridge of his nose, and breathed in slowly, trying to ease the throbbing in his head.

With a shrug, he replaced the glasses and sorted through the stack of mail before him.

Bills mostly.

A card from Lily--he really should call her tomorrow--if only he could summon the energy. He tossed it into the pile of unopened cards that had taken up a third of his kitchen table for months.

Only months. Might as well have been years.

Daniel didn't call Lily the next day.

Or the next.

He thought about emailing her.

He didn't do that either.

Email would insult her.

But, on the phone, she'd get all soft and maternal and ask him how he <u>really</u> was. He would tell her he was fine and she would be determined to get him to open up.

If that happened, she'd realize that there was no point. There was nothing in there.

Nothing.

It didn't hurt any more, living without Karen.

It just was.

He was fine, staying busy at work, and he'd buy new furniture when he had time.

Maybe he should call her, get the revelation over with. Then maybe they could find a way to still be friends. But only if she found a way to be content with his emptiness.

Emptiness was fine.

Really.

Order True Virtue Now!   Virtue.ByJax.com

For special announcements, coupons and insider information, join Jax's email list at books.byjax.com

Made in the USA
Lexington, KY
29 July 2019